WEST

Book Three of the Go Love Quartet

Michael Gills

Published by Raw Dog Screaming Press
Bowie, MD

First Edition

Cover Photo: Lyra Gills

Printed in the United States of America

ISBN: 978-1-947879-09-6
Library of Congress Control Number: 2019931311

www.RawDogScreaming.com

Other Books by Michael Gills

Emergency Instructions

The House Across From The Deaf School: Stories

White Indians: Part 1

The Death of Bonnie and Clyde and Other Stories

Go Love: A Novel

Why I Lie: Stories

Acknowledgements

This novel was written in conjunction with my novel writing workshop, and as such shares energy with the following eight novelists who it was my privilege to join at 4:30 a.m. daily from August 2016 through May 2017: Shaela Adams, Samantha Duzy, Dalton Edwards, James Ehlers, Jenna Garner, Emad Jabini, Madeline Lehman, and Michelle Rohbock.

Huge thanks goes to Daniel Mendoza for reading and editing this novel in manuscript form, and for the encouragement and clarity he showed in doing so. I am grateful to the inestimable Jennifer Barnes, my editor at Raw Dog Screaming Press, and for the support of *15 Bytes*, Dave Pace, Joe Haske, the Goliad crew, Kim Davis and the river folk who keep me mostly honest. As ever, my love and thanks to Jill and Lyra who walked with me amongst the Arizona folk, a lineage writ in dream.

for Jill,
who got me there

and for Lyra, the reason why

Part 1

1. Lara

Daddy keeps the picture of his dwarf uncle in a black Bible under the typing stand in his office. His own daddy's in there, Buddy Washer, and MaMa Josephine, in that envelope fat with pictures of the blood kin he's never met. *Presented to Joey Harvell by Mom Dee—May God bless you all the days of your life. December 25, 1972,* the black book says. I snuck it sometimes, looked into their frozen-grins, and wondered if they'd recognize me. Would they know me as one of their own? Had they secret diseases or lusts or desires that would one day afflict me, so I'd be delirious with whooping cough, grow the tail of a pig and have the condor dream? Who were they that Daddy'd lock them up in that black Bible and act like they never existed? Weren't they my people, too? Sometimes I thought to run off to Arizona and be with them, and they'd roast a goat for me, take me to the dance and call me sister.

Was I a Washer?

Wasn't I?

This was from here to the moon ago, when I thought I knew. When up was clearly up and down was down—good, bad, black, white, richer or poorer, it all made a sort of sense. I was a Utah girl. I went barefoot in the snow. I was not of the "predominant faith." I walked in filth. In shadow. I'd go to hell. I was twenty. A virgin. Millennial. And if you look that up it says: *a period of a thousand years*; *an anniversary of a thousand years*, and *somebody who reaches adulthood in the early 21st century.* I can poke it. My fingertips are calloused. We don't date nor have sex, nor go to dances nor the movies, they say we don't. Our beds have dents in them from our asses where we sit poking our phones, stalking each other day and night and every last one of us is having the most outrageously good time except me. The ones who poke. We are singly unhappy. Forget God. He's dead. *Institutions* give us the creeps. We don't use words like *institutions*. Happy, overrated. Believe me. Understand. Our mamas and daddies don't. Xers, they are themselves the failed offspring of hippies whose *electric Kool-Aid acid trip* and *summer of love* and *give peace a chance* and the *times they are a changing* could have saved us all from a whole lot of hurt, but didn't. I'm part of this story, but the story isn't *me*.

Understand?

Daddy kept the picture of his dwarf uncle in a black Bible. His blood in my veins. Don't lay any baggage on me or mine for saying. How this all came down when I was twenty. No one stays twenty. Do they?

What do you do with the Mormons?

I mean, you can see it in their eyes, judging you the moment you walk into class, that smug turn of the face all through elementary and middle. I grew up on University Street, close enough to hit the U. with a rock. I know that because daddy did it, more than once. It was his party trick, throwing a rock at the University of Utah. And our street was a party street. It got shutdown on either end one Halloween because it was the only place for student hell raisers to go—all those naughty Cinderellas and Hulks and Vampirellas gulping Pabst Blue Ribbon, sucking from a siphon hose then vomiting all over our sidewalk. I grew up like that, beer cans whizzing through the side window at 3 a.m., a coed in white lace lingerie and heels banging our front door after midnight on New Year's Eve when it was five below. My bedroom window faced the street and sometimes I'd lay awake and look through the blinds. House parties for a city block, kids wandering out of one and into another, carrying red plastic cups filled with Purple Jesus and Jose Cuervo, breaking bottles in the middle of the street, fighting, beating the shit out of each other. And once, in the gravel parking slot next door, what happened between that boy and girl on the hood of the car, the street light throwing this pale light, the Friday and Saturday night late shows of my raising. No wonder they could sniff the gentile on me, Mormons.

Close enough to hit with a rock, what Daddy always said.

He was a University man, a history professor, and I first learned to walk outside the museum of natural history, where he'd scrubbed the dirt off this basement window and we could look inside to where these paleontologists excised dirt off dinosaur bones, gluing chips together, so half-rendered beasts reared in the shadowy corners, or that's how it seemed to me, those afternoon walks around campus with the snow falling, Mom on one side, Dad on the other, the hedge of boxwood we had to crawl through scraping our faces.

By first grade, I had no idea I was different from anyone else, but then kids started saying no to my birthday invitations and not inviting me to theirs at all. There was soccer, and when it was my day to bring treats, some kids would turn up their noses, they wouldn't even touch fresh strawberries Mom had dipped in chocolate. It was crazy—I never had one sleep over in my life, except for Ninika Filipovich who was Russian and whose parents liked Daddy because he'd swill straight vodka with them, and eat pickled mushrooms beside a backyard wood fire in wintertime, and Ninika'd kick the shit out of me in bed, so I'd be on the floor—now she's off at Princeton, poor Ninika.

In middle school, everyone was either Mormon, or pretending to be. Non-Mormon's parents were creeps, they killed dogs and ate them, peed off their porches, which I guess is kind of true, we had our yellow spots in the back yard grass. Does that make you corrupt—peeing off your porch?

It all came to a head in seventh grade when I was still pretending, and got invited to seminary across the street from school where they served orange juice and pastry and sang songs, and went to birthday parties and had dates and dances, only there was a rule about how close you could get to a guy, something like half an arm's length, and they had these chaperones with sticks who weren't shy at all about walking up and measuring during a slow dance.

Outside my bedroom window's the football stadium, and up in the tower was where the Mormon dances happened, this huge glass hall with a strobe light and killer speakers, punch and cake. After I got found out, I'd lay in bed and watch them up there, the tiny stick figures lit up by the strobe light, dancing an arms length from one another, the odd gap black between them.

Being a fake Mormon isn't easy.

They have these special underwear with their holy temple name written on them, tops and bottoms, and just how are you supposed to manufacture those? And they know things, like who the Nephites are and the words to songs and prayers and these holy secret rituals like the doctrine of blood atonement, which made it okay to kill a gentile if you baptized them afterward, because the soul would sail off to some special planet where it could live washed in God's love for all time. Photographers showed up at funerals, said *say cheese,* and everybody'd smile. Shit like that. And just let me tell you this. If you're going to fake being a Mormon, don't get found out.

Whatever you do, don't let them find out.

Okay, he's got this study built on the backside of our house, east-facing so the sun comes up in his face. Just off my bedroom, so all those years he'd get up before daylight, go outside and pray by the sage bush, brew coffee, and I'd hear him walk through, unlock the back door and step down into his office where he studied and scribbled maps and legends and notes about the dead dark past, especially about John D. Lee and what happened at Mountain Meadows in New Harmony, where one of our relatives, a Poteet brother, was killed by Mormons dressed as Indians. I'd hear him in there, his typewriter, the odd aroma of burned white sage and cedar.

He'd beat his drum sometimes, fan sage through the cracked door to me, and when I woke I'd walk down the one step with its two-hundred four-leaf clovers underneath it, sit in his lap, hug him, and watch the Hunter rise outside in the east, his club raised, Dad said, to whomp hell out of the bull whose one red eye—Aldebaran— glowed through the blinds of my young life.

That Bible's always been there, beside the wooden desk, on a little typist stand Mom Dee'd bought him when he was eighteen, along with the Smith Corona he let me use as a girl, that Bible's always been there, and more than once on those mornings, before he'd talk me into running barefoot in a foot of fresh snow—the Stepwells are like that, I guess I'm Stepwell just like him—he'd open to Psalms where the folded envelope was tucked, take out the black and white Polaroids and we'd view together the blood people he was born to but had never met. One was of a dwarf on a blanket, his arms raised like a muscle man.

"That's your Uncle Davey," he said when I was twelve. "He was at MaMa's funeral. Remember?"

I didn't. Not the funeral. The white casket, yes, was MaMa hungry in there? I remembered blackberries, a fence line of them blooming white in a field of brown-eyed Susans, the Solgahatchia bottoms, Stepwell land, the cemetery overlooking a lightning struck tree. A gate.

Being hungry.

In my father's office was a map of the universe on the wall we shared. This huge circle with all the constellations in the sky sprawled out on it—Draco the dragon, Ursa bears, Libra, Scorpio and Lupus, dogs and goats and princesses, King Cepheus and his queen Andromeda, the fine harp of Lyra, the whale and the lion and the crab, a white box with black inside for every day of the year, aligned right to left around the big circle, April to May to the June when Uncle Fred came to me in the night, and I was too scared to tell—my first period. Blue lines collide into a cross, straight up and down for the solstices, horizontal for equinoxes, the Lyre constellation I was almost named for south of Polaris.

It had appeared to him, Daddy told me, the month before I was born, when all the visible planets had aligned and a two-tailed comet shone in the west, and he'd prayed that I'd be born happy, that I'd never lose my father or my mother, that I'd believe that love wins all, and that I would not be born a dwarf, that I would find my home.

"So I've got dwarf blood?"

"Yeah," Daddy said.

"My children?"

"Yeah."

"They could be?"

"Dwarfism runs in families. Sometimes it can."

Twelve years old, I could think of nothing more magical than being a dwarf, hitting the road out of Utah, where there were no bimbo blonde Gabby Jensen wearing Jesus underwear to keep asking if I was Mormon, looking down her crinkled nose like she could sniff the filthy gentile in me. Where I'd never have to pretend to quit pretending. They could go jump in the lake every one of them.

I wondered if they were alive, those aunts and uncles on the blanket lifting the dwarf's arms in that strange gold light? Was I like them, did we share eyes, look the same when we cry or smile or laugh or anything at all? Did I take after my great, great, great grandmother Katy who'd once carried a cantaloupe into the camp of Geronimo, the Apache medicine chief who wore around his neck a pouch made from white girl skin? Was I like them? Was I?

June in Utah, before the equinox when I was twelve, the roses had bloomed out front and on the side of the house, big sloppy pink ones that Daddy'd pick, pitch them into the air when Mom drove us to the store for fish, so the petals would shimmy down like pink silver dollars on the windshield, and I'd feel the dwarf blood in me and sing *Oyate wama yanka po,* a snatch of the medicine song from *inipi.* I'd sing it down the steep fall to the valley, pound the drum of my heart which had started to grow inside me, so I could feel it through my shirt now, thrumming, and it was June in Utah and I was twelve.

"And this one is my father," Daddy said.

There he was, posed, one hand on his chin, a good looking man with white teeth on a mountain—how were they always on a mountainside?—with a look that was neither question nor want, but something else. Looking me straight in the eye. Buddy Washer, my grandfather.

MaMa Josephine was taking his picture. She had the light just right on his face. The dwarf had raised his arms like Hercules, and Buddy Washer gazed into that camera, and in turn me, with the confidence of one whose family stands with him. He looks into the camera like a man who has family.

The one of him and Josephine on their wedding day is all different. There's a wedding cake and MaMa has leaned over to cut a slice, and he stands awkwardly at her side, his right hand riding hers on the knife, cutting into the top white layer. This is in Arkansas—Danville, where Josephine's people owned land. The floral shop, Eternally Yours, belonged to Mom Dee and Great Grandpa Si, who'd cut his leg off and got hooked on morphine, who'd played minor league baseball for the Dixie League Little Johns, who would not speak to Buddy Washer, and was not there that Valentine's Day in Danville, Arkansas. Twelve silver forks are arranged on a white tablecloth, and there's a stack of glass plates, a candelabrum with four tapered candles, pink ribbons tied to their bases. They almost named me for her, Josephine, and no one ever had to tell me I looked like her, turn the corner and there she is, framed in glass, myself staring into myself—I can't stand it sometimes, like having a twin. And that day, February 14th, 1959, a Saturday afternoon, she wore white chiffon, a veil that spilled over her shoulders, the white dress low-cut, her lips red, full, and that sad smile. Her Daddy was not there to give her away. She'd wanted a church, the big Methodist across town with a belfry to peel loose after they said *I do* and walked out under the blue sky.

Together, they cut the first slice of a cake that is just off-kilter, Buddy Washer in a bow tie and Air Force uniform. Her father had threatened his life, why?

A shadow from the arched threshold darkens the hallway. He looks scared, Buddy, his hand riding hers on the knife.

She's pretty, I remember thinking, that day when I was twelve and the June sunshine poured through the window overlooking the stadium and foothills, the snow-covered Wasatch. That girl in the wedding gown is pretty, I know her, she dreams of flight like me.

The dwarf on the blanket raises his arms like Hercules—he's cute, really smiling through big white teeth, yucca plants in bloom behind them, cactus, the world half-starved looking for water. On either side, holding his arms up, shirtless men, one Buddy's brother, handsome, white-toothed, a striped bathing suit, and the other, Uncle Earl, Josephine's brother who'd run to Arizona to escape arrest for theft and concealment—I come from outlaws on both sides. A girl, a woman, Buddy's sister Ginger sits on her legs smoking a cigarette, smiling, she looks like Daddy, the sharp nose, the good smile, frozen in space and time in another century, the photographer's shadow long before them, the day grown old.

April, 1960, someone's written at the top, she's pregnant with Daddy the second that picture's taken, where are the two of them, Buddy and Josephine?

Sun lit the top edges of clouds that sailed east that morning when he let me see our long lost people, and then he swept them back into an envelope labeled ARIZONA, folded them into the book of Psalms in the black Bible, returned to the bottom shelf of the typing stand just left of his wooden desk.

I said, "Are there any of your mom and dad and you? The three of you together?"

"I don't know. That's all I got."

"Would you like me to make one?"

He looked at me that morning, and I could tell he was seeing her in me, the way he tilted his head, that odd trace of recognition. There was something else, too. Outside, the foothills rose green, not a mile away as the raven flies. I couldn't know how this mirrored Tucson, how the Catalinas rose from such foothills and valley floor. We were already there, somehow. This was happening in a dream we were having from then and there, where he'd been a baby and they'd buried his birth placenta under a cottonwood tree where Geronimo once rested with his band of ragged people.

"Sure," he said. "All of us all together."

"Me, too?"

He said, "You, too."

Outside, the green lawn where the three of us would lay after dinner and watch the migrating Vs of black-tipped storks, flying high enough to catch the sun, so they glowed like UFOs at night, when we'd lay on our backs and I'd dream of flying with them, past the great lake, to the land of dwarves who looked like me.

"Am I one of you?"

He looked at me with that question in his eyes. And I thought he'd cry, but he surprised me and laughed. "Well of course you are," he said.

And though I never actually drew it out, never fleshed out the vision in my head, I saw them that way, the pretty woman with her white veil and face the same heart shape as mine, the handsome man with the bow tie beneath his Air Force uniform, their hands riding each other's on the long knife, and Daddy there between them, where the cake should be, lit up by the candelabrum, the silver forks and glass plates.

I've never told a soul.

2. Joey

Mama used to tell me how my great, great grandmother, Katy Tremaine, crawled up a fireplace on the day Geronimo and his band of ragged Apaches camped under a cottonwood on the Tombstone farm before their last run at old Mexico. Before the surrender that made them the last Indians in the West to become prisoners of war, sent off to Florida and then Oklahoma where the old medicine man died of pneumonia, his last breath a prayer—*let me go home*. The Chiricahuas had sent an emissary to ask for food, though Mama's telling never included what got sent, beans, jerked antelope, a cantaloupe? There is a Tremaine Avenue in Tombstone today, the family *had* lived there. It *could* be true. And Geronimo did pass that way more than once, pursued by cavalry and banditos and two sovereign governments, so it could be true, Katy with knees bent against her chest, breathing in the dark, soot air on a chill December afternoon, the solstice sun outside lighting up the arms of a sixty foot saguaro they'd decorated for Christmas that year, how the holly strands swayed in the evening breeze, and my blood matriarch asked if she could come down now, and was reminded for the umpteenth time of the leather pouch around the old brave's neck, how it was made from the skin of a white girl named Lucy who'd disappeared last summer. Mama'd tell me the Katy stories when thunder scared me to her bed, on Arkansas nights when the father I'd never met stood in every shadow outside the screen window of the Thayer rent house, the one across from Arkansas School for the Deaf, where the Zebras practiced football on a field right across our street, which reminded Mama of the Jim Thorpe story, another Indian who'd played football and won a shitload of Olympic medals, only they all got took away, and he drowned in Pima County, Arizona where I was born on a Christmas Day after she'd hemorrhaged and these carolers walked in singing *silent night, holy night*.

I picture Mama grown young again, hauling ass across the big heart of Texas with the outlaw who'd fathered me, sage-fragrant wind rushing through the rolled down windows and the world glittery with the thrill of heading west, of bygod *going*, even if it all turned out to be a lie. They'd met under odd circumstances, as it ever is with drop dead love, what she called it, falling for Buddy Washer with his white teeth and combed back hair and rich family back West with their Tombstone ranch and men in the state legislature. Mama was nineteen, had graduated from Little Rock Central the year of the integration and all that mess with the national guard—she couldn't wait to put Arkansas in her rearview mirror for good and ever, a thought that's always weighed heavy on me and was maybe a driving factor in my own escape, though that all comes later. She was tender-hearted like our Lara, believed anything you told her, not a distrustful bone in her body. And he lied up one side and down the other about how his first wife had been killed in a car wreck and their little girl had quit talking, so Mama had pictured herself as the matron saint of all orphaned children, which she sort of became, even though it had all been a load, that and everything else Buddy Washer ever said, except the Geronimo part, maybe, and Katy Tremaine, the odd bedtime story of my lineage. I want to believe.

Fifty years ago it rained like a motherfucker for a whole year in the desert, so by December, when the blizzard blew off Mount Lemmon, the snow blazed like Tilt-O-Whirl mirrors at the Lonoke Country Fair, when the one-armed midget said *goddamnit to hell*, banged his knuckles on the door hinge to make it stay shut, like the sky on fire, like broken water, when I was born, when all this shit starts.

Start it with a birth. Right?

There's this dream-space Mama'd talk about where everything's happened already, where everyone keeps driving past the house they grew up in—you might do this one day, Lara—ease right on past the very window where I sit this second, the sickle moon low in the east, no light yet, I've just stepped out on the dewy grass, tail end August, the Hunter up, Chanticleer clucking on her roost and you gone, your room empty, slowing to look through the blinds or snip snipping forsythia, remember *this* Christmas or *that* Easter, when the dog ate all the hidden Easter eggs and the man of the house got accused of being snockered first thing in the morning, forgetting all his hiding spots. How you can feel the cars pass outside, eyes through the sailcloth curtains where she'd just lit one of those angel mobiles people set up for the holidays, and the pains came on just then, the little bells dinging, that's how she told it, my story. And like I said, it had rained like hell for all of 1960, only it was snow up on

Mount Lemmon where the dwarf wrestlers were holding Pee Wee Ski, with their kegs of beer and bikini bimbos, oblivious to the fact that Mama was hemorrhaging, which I've done since, it can be a big deal, as you know from seeing me on the floor that time, Lara. At Pima County Regional, the surgeon would walk out to the waiting room and say, "The mother won't make it." And the next time he'd say, "The boy won't make it." There sat her who'd be my maternal grandmother, Floradee, with her green eyes shining, having made the drive from Arkansas straight through. And over there, Marion Poteet Stepwell, her ex-husband and my grandsire, with Ruby Jewel, his girlfriend, and her foofy dog, Candy, who had warts. Buddy, he was in jail for smuggling weed in the belly of a Santa suit, but his brother Davey the dwarf was standing in, his little ski suit still unzipped to the chest.

A lot happens before anything happens.

A tinfoil Christmas tree had shorted out in the corner so the room smelled like burnt wire and coffee and rattlesnakes and that desert smell when hard pack's been rained on and the creosote gets full of itself. The room reeked of my people and death and the Christmas carolers had got into the eggnog. The dwarf got the heebie jeebies. The boy would die. The mother would die.

Solstice sun shone on Mount Lemmon, Mount Sinai, temple of God, *round yon virgin o mother and child.*

At 2:32 in the afternoon, Doc walked out and said, "They both made it," and everyone got up and hugged even though they would have killed each other to the bone if another hour'd passed, Davey telling stories about him and The Angel of Sorrow, his card partner on the wrestling circuit, how they feuded with the Sheik and El Diablo, the gay Commancheros. Dee'd roll her eyes and Marion—who folk called Si—belly-laughed just to spite her.

Christmas night, Mama'd hemorrhaged and was whacked on painkiller, so I don't know how she remembers all this, but the sun was setting on Mount Lemmon, shortest day of the year, it had turned red, the color of her blood, the dark river I'd sailed through to this life, and the carolers stuck their heads in the door and sang *silent night, holy night,* and they were drunk and beautiful and dressed as Santa's elves, the holly king reaching the highest note, all the candles burning in his jail cell, and they spoke of Geronimo and how exquisite that last cantaloupe had been, the lush pink flesh of it on the cool green grass. They said that Katy could climb down from the fireplace chimney now, the coast was clear, and a street was named for her and her descendants all down the line, and all the family'd driven off to their hotel rooms for bourbon in plastic cups with a squeeze of lemon and just a shake of water, grandparents now. And my blood father in jail eating his sliced turkey with a plastic spoon, he'd got the call that it was a boy, and *no*, the child was not born with dwarfism, and *no*, the mother would not like to speak to him, and the carolers found the doctor's Puerto Rican rum stash, they moved on to "White Christmas," they sang "Frosty the Snowman" in Spanish.

And she was whacked on painkiller, Mama, but knew that her life had shifted gears, that she'd never be alone for the rest of her life.

"Have you castrated my son?" she asked the attending nurse.

"Do what?" the nurse said.

They lay me on her chest. Our first meeting. "Have you castrated my son?"

"*Castrated*," the woman said.

Frosty se llama, un amigo singular the carolers sang. "Yes. Castrated."

Frosty castrado, they sang. *Un amigo singular*. Security was called. It was too much, the drunk carolers, Frosty Castrado. They tottered out the big double door where Mama's water'd broken. So drunk their breaths might catch fire, they bellowed into the parking lot and disappeared from all this forever on a wave of the obscene *cantar de Frosty castrado.*

It was Mama's story. That's how she told it.

"You mean *circumcise*. Have we *circumcised* your boy."

"Either way," Mama said. "He looks like my daddy."

That's what she said, that she recognized in me the face of her father, that Katy had hidden from Geronimo in a fireplace so he wouldn't make her into a pouch, and that my blood father had once lived in an orphanage, and that had messed him up. She'd never ever let that happen to me. It rained for the whole year before I was born, and the desert bloomed so no one alive who saw it would ever forget. I turned one in Arkansas. O.W. horned his way into the picture. Jimmy and Trace. Arizona receded, flared for a moment, and then went out.

"I get the words mixed up, hon," Mama'd said.

The charge nurse nodded, smiled, wrote something in a notebook. "You might want to hurt him. That's natural. You must fight the urge."

"I'd never hurt my baby."

"Of course not," the nurse had said.

I remember nothing of Arizona or the Washers, Mount Lemmon or the dwarf, it's all a dream to me now. There was something about a window that blew open during a thunderstorm, a shadow framed in lightning, but I turned loose of that a long time ago. When Uncle Earl spilled the beans by saying I had big arms like my daddy, I had no idea. Mama'd thrown everything related to Buddy Washer out of her life except me. The pictures in the black Bible came from Mom Dee, and that only after I was grown enough to ask. She said that when it got bad between Josephine and William— she refused his nickname—Mama had come home off to Arkansas, married O.W., and that was that. They started a new life. It was a good thing. And it wasn't until I skied Monarch Pass, north of Leadville, Colorado, that I understood it was in my veins. The West, it was pulling me back somehow, it had never turned me loose.

3. Joey

Our arrival had coincided with Rodeo Weekend. All through Nebraska into Wyoming the road had climbed steady, then, outside of Rawlins, we'd come upon serious mountains and the highway rose skyward. And just as we passed a giant replica of the Lincoln Monument, the Hertz-Penske overheated and that's how we found ourselves in Rawlins, Wyoming that early evening, where cowboys and cowgirls galloped horseback down Main Street, firing off pistols with the vast Medicine Bow Range behind them as backdrop. Sparks flew from the shoed hooves that rang out like dinner bells. Back home, my sister was forty hours into hard labor, and we'd hit the truck stops and rest areas from one state to the next to get the lastest, how the father hadn't so much as called and how this all reminded Mama of *our* story—how all that Washer business was rearing its ugly head. Renee and I happened on the last hotel room. We still had hooter from Greensboro, and smoked some first thing, looking out the window at the festooned Main Street, at the end of which was the arena where fireworks were scheduled, ground zero Mecca, we'd learn, for gnarl-kneed cowboys from all over Wyoming and the mountain west. I'd been here once with my stepfather, a long-haul trucker, and remembered the antelope, how you'd look out on a mesa and see nothing, then one would flick an ear and a hundred would materialize. But that was a long time ago, and I had changed.

I'd flown out from North Carolina a month ahead with tools and rented the place off State Street on the south side of the tracks, drilled holes and installed new bolt locks on the front and back doors of the second floor duplex, a nice place, really, with a garden already growing out back—the landlord used half the backyard for his personal garden, overlooked by this rundown brick apartment complex with a catwalk off of which Mexican boys peed yellow rainbows, that first week in June, when I'd flown from the Carolina heat to Utah where it was forty-eight degrees that first night and snow shone on the Olympus peak and I drank beer and smoked cigarettes on the front porch at happy hour, thinking about Renee, and our new life—what did I know? I gave the new bolt lock keys to Mr. Hacke, a retired school principal who hired Renee over the phone to be a special ed teacher in Magna, where miners lived, their children not afraid to slap you straight in the face, pull a blade, worse.

Only Mr. Hacke was a dumbass and labeled the keys with our address—1723 East 200 South, in Utah every address has built into it its distance south and east from the Temple, under which is buried, if I understand correctly, a newborn infant sacrificed to each of the cardinal directions—and this heroin addict broke into Mr. Dumbass Hacke's car outside the grocery store and found my keys, nicely labeled, and walked right up to our second floor duplex, fitted the new shiny key into the Schlage bolt lock, walked right in and made himself at home for the month, shooting up, throwing parties, wearing my cowboy boots.

Mr. H. came over to pick tomatoes one afternoon and caught the fucker drinking one of my beers on the back porch, said, "Who the hell are you?"

And this addict, who was wearing my cowboy boots and drinking my cold beer, he said to Mr. H., "Who the hell are you?"

He'd called the police, Mr. H.

The whole block ended up surrounded, TV crews rolling a live shot of this poor fuck in cutoffs and cowboy boots climbing onto the roof, harassed by a helicopter, throwing the boots and weeping and laughing and reciting some flowery nonsense about *here is where I saw the world go gold,* or *intertwine with me in alpenglow,* or *I come to you now with my heart in my hands*, words you no doubt have heard and recognize, daughter, mine.

Of course we didn't know all this until after the fact, on the sunlit afternoon when I drove your mother in the back way, and I watched her heart sink at the sight of the house, the dilapidated apartment next door. Inside, Mr. H. had done his best to clean up, but it was still a mess. The kicker, on the mantle, the ripped open letter I'd written with blue ink on all-cotton paper: *here is where I saw the world go gold,* or *intertwine with me in alpenglow,* or *I come to you now with my heart in my hands*. Underneath this, in a child's scrawl—*ha, ha, ha.* My introduction to Utah literary criticism.

These big ass snow storms would blow in over the lake, wind so hard over the desert that it'd blow forty acres of water off the salty lake so the vegetation would rot and the stench, the godawful stink that gushed over us heralded a lake effect snow. In one twenty-four hour period it dumped 128 inches on Alta Mountain, and a good three feet right outside our door, where it was a misdemeanor not to shovel your entire sidewalk, so the cardiac units were full to the gills before the last flake fell that day.

This was 1993, knee-deep in the dream of Utah, and I was in History for the doctorate. Your mother was teaching over in Magna, miner's kids, a knife fight in her classroom every other week. One kid pulled his pants down and peed on the whiteboard. And the Mormons were so unbelievably weird and fucked up and perverted, so that in my classes all the students' journals were about being molested, and being a prostitute, how the men liked their whores young, and this one guy, he wrote about getting way stoned, driving up to a ward church at night with a buddy who was equally stoned, putting on white robes in the basement and going to the baptismal where a high priest baptized them seventy-five times apiece for the souls of dead Mexicans and Puerto Ricans, El Salvadorans, even Jews. He named names. I mean, this kid, he was put underwater seventy-five times in one night as proxy to claim the souls of the dead. They wrote about wearing Jesus underwear, desire lines cut into them by tight seams, about driving to Nevada to get married and fuck, then getting divorced and driving home all in the same night. All this in a place where a gazillion scornful eyes would turn on you if you lit a cigarette or walked outside with a drink, if you carried a mug of coffee with you to class, for Jesus sake, five Books of Mormon found my mailbox that first semester. We were simply heathen, Renee and me, unclean. Nasty. Scum of the earth. And by the time spring came, the pussy willow bloomed violently between storms when barefoot men mowed their grass, the wheels leaving skinny tracks in the snow.

Why we came west?

Why does anybody go anywhere at all, dragging who they are by the hair of the head, state to state, world to world. Isn't that the old story, how these rag-tag teens fished and hunted their way up the Great Rift Valley where they crossed the isthmus over the Red Sea into what would be the Arabian Peninsula, fanned out across the Ottoman Empire into Europe where they'd evolve into tall Vikings who'd one day sail west for plunder, inhabit Greenland and Labrador, down to the Great Lakes and Appalachians, living on salt cod the Basque had taught them to cure, their hard steel swords and lightning quick boats fulfilling the prophecy of Pahana for the Indians, those who'd fanned east across Asia, across the Bering Straight where Mount McKinley shone snow covered for a thousand miles, followed the woolly mammoth and giant sloth down the Sierra Madres to where the land got skinny, the Caribbean Sea on one side and the Pacific on the other, toward the mountains where God lived and no rain fell for years, down and down to Tierra del Fuego and the Cape Horn that looked out on the Arctic Peninsula, turned around and bygod walked back.

Why?

Did they know, my people, that they drove on asphalt laid over the wagon wheel ruts of the Mormons they mostly detested, and that those very Mormons were themselves tracing the footprints of the Lakota, Crow, Paiute, Blackfeet and Shoshone, following rivers, the Missouri River, Platte, Bitterroot, Green, Colorado, San Juan, Snake, Salmon, the River of No Return.

Had they run from themselves toward themselves, looking for a place to call home, to grow a garden, to raise their kind? I don't know, I can't say. This is the story. For those who scream *Geronimo*. Who die falling. Who go west.

That night in Rawlins, we got drunk and danced the two-step on a saw-dusted floor into a night punctuated by gunfire and the wild neighing of horses. We made love and believed our time was at hand, that we'd finally outrun our lives and things would settle down, we'd put an end to all our fighting and make a baby since we hadn't fucked the dog up too much.

Then I called Buddy.

You see, Lara, it had been in my mind all along, since Uncle Earl let it slip one time that I had big arms, like my dad, and it came as a jolt because it had always been taboo to say anything even remotely related to the dark mystery from whence I come. Not one word from Mama, never. I knew I wasn't O.W.'s, but that's all, maybe the stork *had* brought me, the Easter Bunny or Santa Claus, I had no idea, not until Uncle Earl said it, and I started asking questions. Mama stayed quiet, and I wouldn't think of mentioning it to O.W. Which left Floradee, who broke down and gave me pictures of the Danville wedding, a photograph of Buddy and Mama embracing in the bright sunshine of their wedding day, the photographer's shadow falling at a hard angle over them.

There was a picture of the whole lot of Washers on a blanket on a mountain side, Davey the dwarf in their midst, holding both arms up like a muscle man. A silhouette of my father looked like James Dean. He was handsome. He tried to kidnap me.

And at thirty-three I found myself west and on an evening in early summer when the snow was melting and all the rivers were about to flood, I dialed my blood father from the depths of my past.

He, of course, did not expect to hear from me. The last time we'd had any contact was May 1979 when Mama'd sent him a graduation invitation from Lonoke High, and he'd called her to say he was coming, that he'd be there with a gift of money the family had put together. That night I'd sat on a folding chair in the grass of Jackrabbit Stadium, searching the bleachers for someone who looked like me, but he never came, and time went by, and I might as well have been fathered by the moon.

"Where are you?" Buddy Washer said.

"Utah."

"Where in Utah?"

I said, "A cave in the hills. You still live in a house trailer?"

There was static on the line. It was happy hour. Renee sat across from me wide-eyed. Our dog, Moon, snored under the table. *Telephonitus*, we called it, this drinking and dialing. His voice was familiar. He sounded like Johnny Cash. Mom Dee'd somehow got him thrown in Tucker Prison Farm when he'd come to kidnap me with his brother, the dwarf, who was also a WWF wrestler who worked under the name Dirty Davey or Little Lord Fontelbury. There was a woman's voice, a girl's. "That's your sister," he said.

That I had a sister was news.

"What's your address? I've got something to send you."

I said, "I'm not ready." I gave him our address, the one the heroin addict had read off my bolt lock keys in Mr. Hacke's car.

He said, "Good. I'm glad you called. Utah touches Arizona."

"The Grand Canyon," I said.

"Lee's Ferry," he said. "J.D."

"J.D.?"

"John D. Lee," he said. "Vengeance is mine, sayeth the Lord."

The light had that tint to it that comes in spring, something hopeful, the fruit trees all in bloom, a spring blizzard about to blow everything to hell. I was thirty-four, Renee thirty-five. We'd met over the phone a decade earlier, there had been my brother's car wreck and the move to Carolina. We'd had real fights. We'd been to the clinic. For whatever reason, I'd gravitated toward history, read and reread the Autobiography of Geronimo, dictated by the old medicine chief from Oklahoma territory, where all he wanted in this world was to go home to those mountains north

of Tucson, the San Franciscos, Apache National Forest, the placenta and birth sack
he'd come in was buried under a peach tree, and that was his *omphalos*, the center of
his world, and he could never ever be happy in this life until he went home.

"Was Mama pretty?"

"Very much so," he said.

"What happened?"

"What always happens," he said, and coughed. Phlegm rattled in his throat, his
lungs, the wheezing emphysema that would kill him. "Keep an eye on your mailbox."

I said, "You a smoker?"

Two weeks later a package showed up, mailed from a non-address in Nogales,
Mexico by someone named Socorro. I took it to the garage which was dark and
smelled like gasoline. Mr. Hacke kept tools. I found a box cutter with a silver blade
that slit the cardboard wide open. I smelled a woman in there, her hair. I took it
out in the light. It was an Indian, a ceramic Indian, painted red and yellow, black
and white, ten inches tall, maybe, wrapped in fabric softener sheets for God knows
why. An Indian. Buddy Washer'd sent me an Indian. I sat down in the driveway
and looked at it. There were, of course, little painted moccasins, and feathers, a
headdress. An amulet was painted on its chest. This little Indian had black eyes and
a grim face.

"What you doing down there, Gringo?"

One of the Mexicans was pissing off the balcony, his urine splattering on the
drive. The week before we'd spotted a neighbor kid in the backyard stabbing one
of Mr. Hacke's Hubbard squashes, big as a pregnant belly, slashing it with a pocket
knife. It was a weird neighborhood, a meat house up the street, next to a pottery kiln,
next to a pawnshop, next to a typewriter repair and a tattoo parlor, the mountains
looming up all around, the sun on them, alpenglow.

The Indian had a hole. Between its legs, quarter-sized, dark inside. Scrawled in
a preschool hand around the periphery—*b r a k e.*

I retrieved Mr. H's claw hammer from the garage, broke the Indian in half.

It was a bag of marijuana. A full ounce of skunk weed. There were dark hairs in
it. I could feel its mojo. I threw it in the truck we were packing for our first camping
trip south, down to Torrey, Devil's Backbone, Bryce, where I'd had to wipe my ass
with a red bandana amidst the most amazing rock formations on earth and it got so
cold that I had to bring Moon in the tent, zip her up with me in the mummy bag. A
skunk had sprayed her, so that smell never went away. I'd made a toilet paper bong
and we'd smoked the Jesus out of the pot from the Indian's ass. It had a wild energy

about it, and I first saw southern Utah's moonscape under its influence, and I got to thinking it had me under its power, he had me under his power.

I dug a hole and buried it.

I peed on the hole. I stomped on it. I dug it back up and smoked some more.

Renee didn't know. Everything smelled like skunk in our truck, and we were freezing in flip flops and cutoffs, which no one should ever wear in Utah springtime when snow can fly at any time, and it's thirteen degrees at night in Bryce Canyon, and dope can fuck you up to the point where you endanger yourself, and the ones you love. People die that way all the time in Utah.

We hit Green River and I argued with a man at a gas station that no they did not grow the best watermelons on earth, that those came from Arkansas where people were sane and pronounced their vowels. Due west and south was New Harmony and Mountain Meadows, where a hundred-forty Arkansawyers had been murdered by Mormons under the lead of John D. Lee, I'd learn, godson of Brigham Young, who had himself sent the word to put them down.

They'd set out from Harrison—Poteets amongst them, my people. I did not know this then. How they'd all been head shot, dying for water, carrying a white flag to the well of treachery.

Vengeance is mine, sayeth the Lord. I was arguing about watermelons with the descendent of a mortal enemy. Renee said let's go.

And we hit that stretch from Green River north to Price, that long perfectly straight two-lane stretch called Highway 6, most dangerous highway on earth because speed-freaks would pass you at any time, on either side of the road, they'd blow by semis with a head-on coming at them from the oncoming lane. There were car wreck signs every mile or so, and I'd one day teach a boy who'd grown up in Green River, whose father ran the clinic, who was all the time getting yanked out of bed and driven up Highway 6 in an ambulance where they'd pick up body parts in green garbage bags, take them back home and try to reassemble who was who. We were in that stretch of road, Lara, and we'd just hit a rest stop and huffed the hooter, the skunk. On the road again, flying, Renee behind the wheel, The Grateful Dead playing "Fire on the Mountain" real loud and I felt it, that manic energy from the dark place in the Indian, the cavity, a woman's hair was in there—Mama's?—it was bad medicine, wasn't it? I threw it out the window then, on Highway 6, between Green River and Price, and we kept on driving toward Soldier Summit and home.

Two months later, the amniocentesis showed a girl. *You.*

We never looked back.

4. Lara

You used to take me there for my birthdays, usually after happy hour when it was getting dark, and you'd haul off and drive me to Regional where we'd park underground and walk the hallway lined with paintings of nuns, those stern, wimple-draped faces, through the double doors of the maternity ward with its big glass window looking onto babies with names written in magic marker scotch-taped to the cribs, some hooked up to machines and incubators, then we'd walk past the huge desk with its attendants and dry board and names of expecting mothers and their attending physicians, checks in boxes for meds, hours in labor, who knows what all, and you'd somehow sweet talk those ladies into letting us into the room, the one at the end of the hall on the right with its windows overlooking the rose garden fountain and statue of Mary, babe in arms, and we'd sit on the bed in the room that looked Victorian, everything masquerading as something else, where you'd smile and breathe deep—security about to burst in and arrest us any second—look me in the eye and say, "This is where you were born, Lara. Right here."

It was a troublesome birth, mine. Forty hours on Pitocin before Mom ever dilated an inch.

You listened to Jazz, John Coltrane, maybe, the narcotics had her laughing, Mom, a regular party, the sun bright outside the window on the withered rose garden that was built in 1959, the year of her birth, a good sign, no? Backgammon, dominoes, five card stud, day went to night went to day. Outside, beside the frozen fountain, seagulls flew above an old man chunking bread. You craved pizza, Mom chomping ice cubes, toxemic, laughing then crying then laughing. You always told me how the room accelerated, how you walked down to that exact spot and prayed at the smoker's ashtray, blood bags were drawn, the caesarian talk dismissed, then an epiduralist—a white-masked shaman, you called him—slipped an eight-inch needle into my mother's seventh vertebrae.

The full wolf moon. A ruddy midwife shared a clove cigarette with you outside the downstairs lobby. Just outside the double glass doors, she said, "You watch and see. Look out." A wisp of smoke seeped through the gap in her front teeth. "All these spring-bred babies? They wild to be born. Little wild things," she said.

You'd read the books, attended birthing classes where young Mormon couples were red-faced that everyone knew that'd made nookie, nookie. Mostly, during the classes, you and mom were fine, the best breathers in the E-wing, only Mom went toxemic mid-way through the third trimester. Blue ankles, chills, feeling like her eyes were about to burst out of her head.

You'd tell me the old story, the way your mama'd told it to you, the odd bedtime story of my birth, like it was somehow different, a moment that, if understood, would be a key to the shining secret of this life. That's how you told it, slurring sometimes.

"Right here," you'd say, slap the bed with a flat palm. You'd brought pillows from home, a flute with a broken valve, Mardi Gras beads and lip balm, you moved in, took up residence. And that full moon night when I came, the place blared with bodies breaking out of bodies. Shrieks tore through the walls and you swear to God somebody screamed, *"Goddamn you. I'll cut it off. Before you do this to me again, I'll cut it off."*

Mama?

I came squalling at 2:52 a.m. You counted one, two, five, seven on Mom's belly, her pushing, determined, real. A piece of my head shone through, the size of a nickle, a quarter, a fist, *one two three good good.* When I screamed, the midwife said, "She's a feisty one," so that's what you'd always tell me, that I came out kicking, that I'm a feisty one.

Is that true, Dad? Our history?

You held me in your arms. Mom'd split. You rocked me and hummed to me while the midwife cut flesh away, stitched the wound. I know the melody, sweet and sad, I hear it sometimes and think of you.

"I like that humming," the midwife said. "Most people are watching a rerun of Gomer Pyle when the baby comes."

We are three. Birth starts us.

In January, a Friday, light charcoal sky with corn snow, just a flurry, passing. The doors swing outward, and a light snow snows down the low gray sky outside this hospital in Utah which, yes, touches Arizona. With me, the prophesied circle of your life—the dark maze with a man at its center, closes. You wheel us out under the big sky. Our breaths, the three of us breathing, the single breath rising, converging.

A front skirts the lake. A squall line. Sometimes you forget this.

The air is wet, it carries the lake where wind blown over the salty shallows away from rotting vegetation smells like carrion. Our truck was silver, nearly new, you'd washed it. You'd cut your hair, a fresh haircut MaMa Josephine would say when she saw our picture. There was the exhaust smell, and I see you through the tiny window. Mom's smiling and afraid and I'm invisible beneath blankets, the white cap covering my misshapen head and tree-black hair the length of a hand. Seconds, only seconds. My first photo, the nurses eye to the lens, and the Pitocin oozes from Mom's skin, every pore giving thanks for fresh air, and this is the moment, the truck doors are open and the engine running. You take me home.

Home. You'd made the sign: *Welcome Home Mommy and Lara.*

Only this one time, when I'd just turned eighteen, they'd remodeled and the double doors wouldn't open and you forced them. Inside, a security guard said, *Stop! Don't go any further.* He touched his pistol butt. Only it was Bill Salt, your river friend, and you told him it was my birthday, that this was a thing we did. Mom had cake waiting at home, carrot with Italian cream cheese icing, homemade pasta with pesto, and you'd made bread. Bill, he let us keep going, past the glass that looked onto the babies, up the hardwood aisle to the desk of names. Mom thought we were crazy. I thought we were crazy too—people didn't do this, barge into the maternity ward. You said it was my *omphalos*, what the hell was *omphalos*? the center of my universe, you said, like you whose birth placenta was buried under a cottonwood tree on Tremaine land south of Tucson. I would never ever, ever be happy until I walked on this piece of earth. The woman behind the desk, the attendants, they were not happy to see us coming, and when you spoke, explained that I was born in that room right over there and could we please go in, that they always let us go in, they said the room wasn't there anymore, that it had been remodeled, *no one will ever be born in there again, sir, I'm going to have to ask you to leave.*

"It's her birthday. Her 18th birthday."

"Sir," the woman said. The other called security.

Bill Salt pretended he didn't know you. He said, "I have to ask you to come with me."

"You can't take this away from her. It's not yours to take away."

Bill took one arm, I took the other. "This way, sir. I'm sorry."

I said, "Come on Dad."

Behind us the women poked the hell out of their phones, and the police were waiting for us behind the double doors, beyond the babies, and I was afraid you would fight them, that they'd shoot you and my birthday would always be the day you died, in a maternity ward for God's sake. Handcuffs shone on their belts. There were three of them. One had a Taser drawn, and I was so scared. "Just let us go home," I said.

Bill said, "I've got this gentlemen. This one is entirely mine."

"You sure, Salt?"

"Yeah," he said, and the cops left. The nun paintings were blue in the light, they looked haunted, like they'd seen the shadow of death and given in to it, like there was no light outside or a tomorrow, or any happiness anywhere to be found, like I'd never fall in love or get married or have children or text Jackson Tripp at night when the full moon shone in my window and I tingled from head to toe. On my eighteenth birthday, the nuns sucked me into their black hole.

Bill walked us out to the car. You let me drive. "I'm sorry," you said. "They've always let us in."

"I don't need to go there anymore Dad." I said it.

You said, "What?"

"It's just a room. I don't need it."

And you looked at me like I'd said the most hurtful thing, and we'd driven home and had my cake and cold pasta. Years later, after my first day and night on foreign soil, when I literally ached for the Wasatch to rise up around me, I'd realize that you weren't going for *me*, our yearly returns were never about taking me to the exact spot of my birth—to my center. That day in January, when you watched me come into the world, when you held me in your arms and hummed that sweet sad song, you'd found your place. I'd never thought of that, and I bet you haven't either. All those years ago, when MaMa Stepwell found out the worst of your daddy's lies, when she ran like crazy from Arizona and did not say goodbye, she didn't realize that it was the center of your universe she was running away from, and that there'd be this hole in your heart always until you went back, and maybe there was no going back.

All you'd ever wanted was home.

Is that what my birth room was for you? Is that why my history's so that it entwined with all the histories in your head?

Is that it—*West*?

5. Buddy Washer

Never looked back my ass. You've been looking back your whole life, and there was once in a thunderstorm in Arkansas when I'd found you, found which room they had you sleeping, and the window was open. Your crib was just inside, blue with white chiffon from our wedding, Josie was good with stuff like that. There was a mobile, little bears or squirrels or something, and every now and then a gust of wind would make it tink, and I could hear your grandmother Dee and Josie arguing in another room, the kitchen, maybe, which faced Thayer Street where I'd parked way off by the Fair Grounds with Davey, your uncle. There was thunder booming and lightning, that Arkie boondocks smell, and it was dark, so no one could see me there behind the bush, and I could see you through the screen, smell your skin, hear you breathing, my own flesh and blood, and that was hard to take. You got a kid? You want to stand outside that screen and feel what I felt—she stole you from me, took you in the night and never said bye, kiss my ass, nothing. People've been killed for less than that. There are laws. You can't just take a man's son and jump on a Greyhound bus and disappear. I knew she'd run back to Dee. The house wasn't hard to find. She was an auditor for the state, worked at the Capitol down off Markham on 7th. So I'd followed her home that day, and sure enough, there was Josie, and you in a bedroom with an open window and a storm was blowing in, a real doozy.

You were awake. It was April 5th, a Thursday, and we'd driven all night across Texas, up through Gurdon by Lake Ouachita where your granddaddy lived in a trailer on the water; that'd put you around sixteen months, just starting to walk and talk and know people that night when you'd be mine again. You were awake. You saw me out there, my face. You sat up. You said *Daddy* and reached both hands out to me. Dee and Josie were fighting off somewhere in the house with its dipshit locks a duck could pick with its bill. And you reached to me, said "Daddy."

"That's right son. It's me. I love you."

The wind was blowing. It started to hail that second, little pea-sized hunks thunking off the roof. The screen was one of those old-fashioned jobs with hinges and a little hook through a rivet on bottom. Not a problem. You see, what you do is take a paper clip bent into a right angle and poke through the mesh down low and pry the hook from the rivet, so that's what I was doing when the hail and this hellacious wind came up, and you reached your hands to me and smiled so wide and said, "Daddy," and God and Jesus how I'd missed you.

You sat up. They had you in a blue bouncer, a little stuffed dog you called Fido that you'd vomited on about a hundred times. I remember you smiled, this big, real smile that comes from my people where you belong.

I said, "Joey. I love you."

And you said, "*Dat. Luh you.*"

You weren't scared of me. You knew me as your daddy. You'd waited for me.

The latch had come free, and I lifted the screen on its little top hinges, sat it on top of my head and reached through. The air smelled like thunder, the lightning on your face, your smile. Daddy's come for you.

The lights flickered, came on.

"The screen's blown off," Dee said. How close I got.

How's that for looking back?

Back at the car, Davey'd sacked out. I was soaked to the bone. We drove over to Pleasure Lanes on Asher, rolled a few games, and Davey arm-wrestled this dude for a pitcher of beer.

1962, I was twenty-five. Twenty goddamn five. What kind of world is it where a man has to cross Texas and steal his son back in a hail storm? Say?

Your Mama'd started painting birds. Did you know she painted birds? With your face on them? Beat all. The window slamming episode got you moved somewhere else in the house, and the only way I could get close, the only thing I could think of was to deliver the mail. What would you do? Somebody take that little cutie of yours, haul her off to who knows where? It's really not a bad job, walking outside under the good sun, even though the Natural State's a hot bastard even in spring, and that's saying something given I hail from desert. And you can find any kind of uniform at Goodwill. I knew this basketball player got hisself a cop outfit and a bubble gum light, a silver badge, he drove around pulling people over and writing them tickets, made 'em pay on the spot, called hisself the Sheriff. What I'm saying is that becoming the Postman's not the hardest thing on earth, much easier than, say, becoming an electrician, which I did for your mother way back when, and so what if I played snooker at Charro's some days? Who said life has to be such a goddamn godawful load of crap every day the sun comes up?

Say?

The mail part was a little tricker, I mean having stuff to deliver so it'll at least look like you're who you say you are, if anyone asks or watches, which they mostly don't. I mean, who cares? I bet my ass that dressed as a postman you could walk up to anybody's front door, and, if the timing was right, they'd make you a sandwich and pour you a knock of whiskey, give you a wrapped up gift with a bow on it at Christmas time—a high dollar present if you hit the Heights or Cammack Village, the motherload over in Pleasant Valley, those houses butt up against the country club, stuff you could pawn for real money if you know what I mean.

But you have to have the goods. Junk mail's a piece of cake. Go to the bowling alley, it's everywhere. Stacks of flyers for handyman work and gun safety classes, baby-sitting services and AA meetings, stacks of coupons and happy hour invites, lost dogs and cats, used prosthetics and wheelchairs for sale, junk's easy. Having real-deal letters now, especially one from a judge ordering custody of a child on notarized stationary, now that's technical. Davey knew this guy who'd wrestled out of Pine Bluff, call him Scoggins, who did that kind of work, but that cost us an arm and a leg. I wrote a whole slew of return to sender not at this address envelopes, but you still had to have stamps. Ever try buying stamps for, say, two hundred letters? Know what that takes? So we had to ring Scoggins up again and pay an arm and a leg for one of those nonprofit stamps and who knew that was a federal offense? I mean who goddamn walks around with that knowledge in their head?

So I'd figured out the letter and mail end of the deal, had my postman outfit and set to figuring a route that would not interfere with the real postman, who turned out to be a woman, and she didn't give two shits if I walked right with her, which I did because she was on the pretty side, long in the tooth, but pretty. This real postwoman let me walk with her, and even once her boss came and she still let me do it, said I was in training and she was teaching me to interact with clients, which I did, so I started feeling like I really was a postman. She let me drive her truck some days. And then she said she felt bad one day about two weeks into it, she had a tummy ache, Miss Patty, would I deliver today. Could I do it? She trusted me with her whole load, Miss Patty.

Davey'd scored us a place to crash out back of Pleasure Lanes, so there was usually food, popcorn always, and beer, sometimes cold. Who likes showering for work with a water hose? Life's not perfect.

So I delivered mail for real, and my route ran straight by 1723 Thayer, a right side duplex in front of which your mother, Josephine, painted birds with your face on them. I think the heat and ticks make Arkies crazy. So that's what she was doing that April afternoon when I served Scoggins' court order on her, saying that she was to release a certain Joey Washer to his rightful custodian and blood kin, William Lewis (Buddy) Washer, or face criminal charges in the COURT OF PULASKI COUNTY, notarized on 15 April 1962, so help me God.

"Josephine?"

"Buddy."

"How you been?"

She said, "Better than I used to be."

"I'm glad for you."

"Me too."

"Who fixed your broke tooth."

She didn't answer me that, about the front tooth got chipped by accident. "And Joey?"

"Better too. He's better."

"Sure is hot."

"What do you want?"

"You still drawing them birds with his face on 'em?"

"You're impersonating a postman."

I showed her the letter then, the one from Judge Justice Honorable Ronald E. Nehring, who'd written papers on her. "Maybe I really am the postman."

You'd climbed up in her lap. You wanted to come to me. You reached for me and smiled and said you loved me. It was a green bird, a hummer with this long beak below the blue eyes I give you. It wasn't yet five, happy hour rolling in, the real live mail truck parked round the bend, keys jangling in my pocket.

"This letter's for you. Judge signed it."

She said, "My daddy'll cut your head off."

I said, "I love you."

"Your head. He'll cut it off."

"In your heart you know it's true. You know that you two are my family. My *only* family. I want you back."

She was thinking about it. Her and Grandma Dee fought tooth and nail. I mean we were this close to hopping in that mail truck, the three of us, both doors wide open, driving on off to Texas with the wind whipping our hair and that good sunshine in our eyes and we'd camp under the stars and I'd make chili dogs and home fries and we'd sleep in the truck bed and there'd be checks mailed to people we'd open and cash and no one would ever know. There'd be fields of flowers with fat creeks all lazy through them. I'd teach you to fish and she'd nap on the banks, wave sometimes, the light streaming down on her hair. We'd be happy.

"Leave. Get on out of here."

"I have rights. Judge says so."

"Get your sorry ass away from here. I'll kill you."

"You already have. Judge says give him over."

Dee, your grandmother, she drove up that second like she always did and ruined our make up—I was this close, this goddamn close. She screamed those things your ears should have never heard, nor should any boy have to watch his daddy handcuffed, shoved in a car that way, driven off to Tucker for the rest of his life, maybe. Goddamn go to hell.

Turns out it all happened during a tornado, hit a bank down to Mount Ida where your grandpappy lived, killed sixteen, served the fuckers right.

She worked for Faubus, Dee did. Your grandmother was close to the man, I don't know how. And he's nobody to fuck with, Faubus. Anybody'll call the National Guard out to do battle with the Federal Government just to keep a couple black kids out of school. That's the thing about you Arkies, you're all shithouse crazy, all of you, and maybe Floradee most of all, have me thrown under the bus like that, what did I ever do to deserve that? Goddamn Tucker Prison Farm picking peas? Give me a break, son? Can I call you that, *son*? You know you got a brother, a Mexican brother and sister. Hey, guess what we named your sister? Guess. We named her Josie, well Josephine altogether. Your bubba's named Roberto, he got his finger cut by a power saw one time, index on the right hand. Hear you're missing the same. What are the odds of having two sons by different mothers, both of them had their index fingers on their right hands cut off? It's the dwarf blood makes things like that happen. Cousin Joquita, she was born with the tail of a pig, and Davey's little boy had horns. Had to have 'em sawed off. Mama's daddy had three testicles. How 'bout your little girl, little cutie with that cowlick sticking up, anything peculiar with her? Maybe I meet her one of these days—all of you. Can't hide forever.

Forgery is of course a felony in Arkansas and the cops had me flat, cuff me right in front of you and the world, shove me in that backseat and drive me away and the letter signed by Judge Justice Honorable Ronald E. Nehring, a name Davey's Pine Bluff buddy stole from a phone book in Kalamazoo, Michigan, of all goddamn places. And Miss Patty and her tummy ache, she said I slipped pills into her Co-cola and stole the whole kit-n-kaboodle, tied her up in her bedroom and made off with the mail truck, the lying bitch. My story's way better, say?

So they had me clean.

And your grandma Dee? She threw in attempted kidnaping, tracked ole Scoggins down in Pine Bluff. He plea-bargained for immunity so they got the whole nine yards, and the whole thing went federal, a double felony now. Davey posted bail but it got turned down cause Dee claimed I'd flee, that I'd served time before, that I was a danger. She'd hired this lawyer, put the call in to Governor Faubus, and I got monkey-rigged to Tucker. Three weeks, that's all it took. Put that in your pipe and smoke it. Your grandmother Dee, she got me locked down for two years at Tucker Prison Farm where they grown peas, purple hulls, miles and miles and miles of peas. You ever pick peas? Ever pick a peck of peas? In August? In Arkansas? For a long time I'm thinking, I owe that lady one, your grandmother Dee. Then Josie went off and married that truck driver. When my time was done, I rode the bus home, and I don't ever think I'll go to Arkansas again.

One more thing.

You got a kid. You know you go through your whole life thinking *me, me, me, me, me, I, I, I, me, me, me.* Then this kiddo gets born, and all of a sudden it's *you, you, you. Us.* And every last wrong ever been done to you don't matter anymore, you've got a purpose in life, and this little being who has inside of them everybody you ever loved on this earth, they reach for you and they smile and they call for you and they love you no matter what. And it makes you a better person. Tell me you don't know what that feels like, to be loved like that. You know. I know you know. Your mama and I, we had a home. I taught her how to refry beans, make corn tortillas and guacamole. We grilled the goat. She liked music, Elvis. On paydays I'd broil napalitos and anchos, pork for carnitas and frybread and we'd dance by the radio in the living room and she'd smell like lime juice and frybread and we'd hold you between us and you'd laugh and this was real, I swear to god. We took pictures. She show you the pictures?

I made some mistakes. The thing with Socorro in Sonora, who saw that coming? The weed bust? And when work ran out, they turned loose all the ground electricians first because we cost them the least—what was I supposed to do? Just come home and say I had no job, we had no income, that we'd have to live on dirt, my new family?

At least at the snooker table I had a chance. And I won some there too, so it's not like what you've been told. And what else is there to do while your hustling snooker than knock down a beer or two, let the other guy think he's got you now, just one more beer and this snooker shark's going to lose his touch. You see what I mean?

Another week or two and we'd of been in the clear. We were just that close. She hauls off and steals you to Arkansas, doesn't even tell me goodbye? And that note, was that supposed to make me feel better? Make it okay?

I crossed three states to get you back and what'd it get me—two years at Tucker. So seems to me like the chickens, they gonna come home to roost—sometime they will. So Josie goes and marries that truck driver and next thing I know I get a notaried letter says:

NOTICE

IN THE PROBATE COURT OF PULASKI COUNTY, ARKANSAS

IN THE MATTER OF THE ADOPTION OF JOEY STEPWELL WASHER—NO. 44364.

William "Buddy" Washer and all whom it may concern, take notice that on the 9th day of March, 1966, a petition was filed by O.W. Harvell and his wife Josephine Harvell in the Probate Court of Pulaski County, Arkansas, for the adoption of a certain person named JOEY STEPWELL WASHER. NOW, unless you appear within thirty (30) days after the date of this notice and show cause against such application, the petition shall be taken as confessed and a decree of adoption entered.

R.S. Peters, Clerk. Stella Jones, D.C.
3-23 Wed2t.

Now, let me ask you this. Go on a picture yourself standing in the door of that Utah house you live in now. In your hand is a notaried letter just like the one you just read, only instead of my name, it's yours, and instead of your name, your daughter's— Lara Summer Faye Harvell. Pretty little thing. Why, how does it feel down in your gut? What thoughts go through your head? Son? What you thinking? What are you willing and not willing to do to get sweet thing back?

Would you cross state lines? Consider kidnap?

Would you risk prison?

Say, son? For that daughter who you love, your one baby, would you burn down somebody's house? Take life?

6. Joey

Near the end, light hurt Mama's eyes. She wore smoky glasses around the house on a street in Lonoke, Arkansas that had once been an orchard, and the lamps stayed off all day, she never turned them on. Through four governors, she'd run the forms management and printing office for the state and her office won yearly prizes at the end of term awards ceremonies. She was liked.

Lifelong friends called her regularly, and, as much is possible for a human being, she'd stopped dwelling on Jimmy's car wreck, the words he'd last spoken to her, the state trooper's knock on the door at four a.m. Maybe she'd stopped seeing him in his silver casket, I never will. Then her lupus roared from remission to full flare, and her retirement party was a rushed affair with paper cups and a cardboard memory book, a plaque that sits on top of my bookshelf now: *Presented to Josephine T. Harvell, In Recognition of Exceptional Service To The Department of Finance And Administration 1981-1997*. It's shaped like the state of Arkansas, a keyhole, the plaque, has a little sticker on back that says *Congratulations From Discount Trophies*.

We met her at the airport, Renee, the baby and me, on a June afternoon in Utah, the sun white glare off what was left of the mountain snow. The highway had been ripped up for resurfacing. Traffic was bad. We'd argued some while creeping on the side roads where farmers sold Bing cherries by the bucket on plywood stands. We were late. I got out at the terminal and hurried away while Renee parked in short term and carried our daughter to the gate. The plan was to be the smiling, well-dressed family, come to greet MaMa. I'd made a welcome poster of an airplane over the Great Salt Lake, with *We Love You* written across the width of silver wings, followed by each of our names in the clear window slots. Home, it was planted in the middle of our fresh cut lawn, where wild roses bloomed on thorn branches.

I saw my mother before she saw me, by the gate, through the last of the wheelchair passengers. Her face was swollen behind the dark glasses. She was tired. I'd expected Mama to be tired. But she was something else, too.

"Mama," I said.

She smiled, and it was real.

"Have I missed the Olympics? I've decided to be a ski jumper." We hugged then. Behind the dark glass, she cried.

We lived then, the three of us, on a street near the University, in the foothills where ancient glaciers flowed down from the mountains, so that if you dug holes for fence posts you'd hit this layer of boulders and have to use a pry bar or forget about it. From the front porch on a clear day we could see Nevada to the west, the valley of prehistoric Lake Bonneville, its shoreline cut into the panorama of foothills. Mountains rose up sheer from ocean, twelve, thirteen thousand feet so that storms blew in from the desert, dragged moisture from the lake, and dumped blizzards that staggered the mind—ten, fifteen feet sometimes with drifts tall as church steeples, and the sun would come out blinding, and even then the cold enough to freeze lips together on an afternoon in January. *Utah*, an Indian word for place where there are mountains. Where a mother stork flapped in on black-tipped wings, alabaster and obsidian at first light of first day, the Utes say, the first man and woman between their beaks.

Some of the rundown houses on our street had couches in their front yards where students and frat boys and ditsy coeds did beer bongs after football games at the stadium that was near enough to hit with a rock. The other houses people like us had bought, the only properties this high up that normal money could buy, and we'd got in cheap from the crazy recluse who'd nailed all the windows shut and lived on cornflakes and Carnation milk. Our house faced south, across the street from a thirteen story retirement home called Friendship Manor, only the *o* and *r* had shorted out on the neon sigh, so it read *Friendship Man*, which Mama thought was funny.

"That's the kind of place I'll end up at," she said.

Renee'd carried Lara in the back way, our black lab bounding out under the blooming pear and apple. I took one of Mama's arms, lifted her out of the backseat and let her brace on me. We were a mile higher than the delta she'd departed that morning, so the air was thin—giddy in her lungs, each breath like a sip of champagne, she claimed.

"Only my sign will say *Enemy Man, House of Foe*."

She was heavy. Her hair smelled like our house back home, and I felt real guilty for moving west and leaving her to fend for it with only my sister and O.W. who'd let the run over mailbox stay that way for six months, so the postwoman had to get out of her truck, pick up the box with its silly red flag bent in half, stick the phone and gas bill inside with the rest of the junk, shut the thing up and drop it by the roadside, so Mama'd wheel herself out and repeat the same gestures day in day out.

Out of breath on the back patio, I felt her heart beat in the one arm stretched around me. She was breathing hard. The wrought iron table had a rock arrangement on it from the south desert.

I sat her down there, just off the spring garden. When I got back with her bags, she hadn't moved.

"How about we just sit here for a minute?"

I said, "Sure, Mama."

"Good."

"Can I get you some ice water. Are you hungry?"

Across our narrow street, a painter was putting the last licks of Pioneer White on the wood frame bungalow an elderly Mormon couple rented to newlyweds who'd fuck like badgers, give birth, move to a bigger house, and thus make way for more newlyweds. They were good natured people, mostly, the Mormon newlyweds, though one wife had on purpose run over her husband's leg with a moving truck.

"I'd like that, sweetie. It's time for my pill."

"Hello out there." Above us, framed in the screen window, Renee held sixth month old Lara.

Both of them smiled down at us.

"*Da, da, da, da, da, da,*" Lara said. They'd been the first words out of her mouth. "How sweet," Mama said. "Come say hey to MaMa, cutie pie."

She was pale, Mama, and the dark glasses. She loved ice water, all her life she loved ice water. I heard them out on the patio while I cracked ice. It was happy hour. Renee'd opened wine. I poured whiskey, added another dollop, a squeeze of lemon. Then I sliced radishes, pickles, black olives and added a hunk of cheddar to the board. I knew she hadn't eaten well, not for a long time, and the lupus had come back on her, she'd had a time.

Lara's in the wind-up swing. The fence line roses had bloomed. We were in the backyard, on the patio and across University Street the painter had rolled it up, the place was done.

Mama'd taken her pill.

I said, "How is everyone?"

Mama said, "Good. Daddy's playing for the Club Championship next month and Mom Dee has got over the flu." She took the glasses off, and there she was, her face was puffy, but it was her. "I'm good and bad. What's that I smell?"

"Renee's making pizza. Smells like sausage."

"She *makes* pizza?"

I said, "How's Trace?"

Mama said, "Fine."

"Dougie?"

Across the street, the house was going gold. "He's my special boy."

"Do you ever talk to him about his dad. Or does Trace?" We make a triangle, the three of us: Lara, yawing in the windup swing, and Mama at my side, like her all grown up, seeing me through eyes the color of plowed earth.

"Blake? We don't talk about him."

Bells chimed up at the University, one hour sliding into the next. The swing had put my daughter to sleep, it happened every time.

I said, "That's not right, Mama. Not telling the child about his father."

And so I again touched the old wound, how I'd never met my father, the taboo of my life.

She looked at me then, as if I'd struck her. Her chin quivered. "You hurt me so bad, Joe. I need to go to bed now."

She got herself up the stairs, and in the bathroom I could hear her crying. I had my whiskey, and then another. And when it got dark, a street light shone down on the newlywed house, freshly painted. The artificial light on new paint was fierce—it hurt to look at.

It was the saddest light I'd ever seen.

A massage had been arranged for that Saturday at House of Healing, a school downtown where student practitioners did Swedish style at discount rates. Our argument from the night before was forgotten—if we held grudges, we never mentioned them. They'd burned incense and people were examining crystals in the adjoining shop, everyone sipping green tea and nodding just a little to the zither and chime and percussive thumps coming from speakers hidden in nooks and crannies set to the *Earth Resonance Frequency*, the clerk who took my money said, *for deeper relaxation.*

Mama's lupus had come on hard after Jimmy died, super-fueled by grief and hopelessness and the need to scream her head off at stupid people saying stupid things as stupid people are apt to do with the best of intentions. First came the butterfly rash across her face, a pink spray of delicate veins that blossomed across both cheeks and the bridge of her nose, and that burned some, though there were creams and such to make it better. Her forearms flared like she had measles—I've passed these through blood to Lara, tiny dots that signal rheumatoid arthritis, lupus, maybe—so we've skipped a generation. But all this was kiddy cake to what happened next, *the wolf that eats itself* for which it was named, when her body's immune system began to attack itself, so her joints would swell and crack, and she'd cry and moan and scream sometimes. And if anything happened to upset her while this was going down, say she'd fall out of her wheelchair while powering out to the knocked down mailbox stuffed with Piggly Wiggly flyers and coupons for Popeye's chicken, the effect could loop in on itself and intensify, and then she'd have to go to the ER, where they'd one more time go through the forty thousand tests to determine that *yes*, she *did* have lupus, both systemic and discoid, and it appeared to be in full-flare. They'd put her on morphine, and might as well have put her on the moon. Lupus was a bitch, but morphine was worse.

Our names were called by a masseur in blue scrubs, and he motioned for us *both* to follow, the first sign of what was to come. I'd been to House of Healing before. When my back went out, we got insurance to kick in and I was allowed massage for a month, these hour-long sessions when they'd spray essential oils and I'd strip naked, get under a warm sheet, and this strong-handed girl named Crystal would come in on a thrum of music, pull the sheet down to my waist, and touch me in a way that eased my blood, the injuries of my upbringing, the anger and loss and hurt of being. Minutes stretched deep. I'd hear the swish of lotion rubbed between her palms, then warm on my flesh. After, she'd let me get dressed and bring me cold water, tell me to drink lots for twenty-four hours which I did. That's how it was supposed to work. Once in Monterrey, Renee and I had a couples massage for our anniversary, but it was usually alone, in a room that smelled of lavender, Indian music, zither and chime.

This masseur in blue, he led us into a room where there were two tables separated by a sheet hung from a rod in between, where stood a second student masseur who said, "How are we doing today?" motioned for Mama and whipped the sheet shut between us.

We were instructed to undress to whatever degree we were comfortable with, get under the sheet, wait for them to return, adjust the prop to meet out faces. What needed immediate attention? What part of us hurt the most?

Six feet away, Mama groaned. Under my sheet already, I heard the student walk in on her. "Oh, I'm sorry, honey," he said. "Take your time."

I was a little hung over. I told the masseur I hurt all over, and he said to tell him if his touch was too strong. There was the lavender smell, the beat of drums. I thought of Renee home with Lara, how we'd given Mama our bed and slept in the basement on a futon, and she'd gone along with it, no problem. We'd moved west twice now, once as thirty-something outlaws in love with the space and light and blue sage growing wild in fields of antelope overlooked by saw-toothed mountains. And a second time in retreat from Arkansas, west, toward hope and home and family. Renee'd grown up military. Rootless, the wind could have swept us anywhere. Bonnie and Clyde they'd called us in Carolina, because she looked like Faye Dunaway, and I'd had run ins with the law.

The masseur folded my right arm behind my back, and he touched the seam where a surgeon had once reattached the index finger on my right hand, so there was a flash of pain. *Jesus*, I said.

On the other side of the sheet, Mama screamed. "I'm sorry," she said.

"No, I'm sorry, honey."

"It's me," she said. "I'm a mess."

"Does this hurt," my masseur said. He dug his fingertips into my right scapula. The pain was sudden. It radiated. Eleven on the scale of one to ten. "No," I said. "You're fine."

I deserved it. Go ahead and kill me.

"What exactly's wrong with you, sweets?"

Mama's sheet rustled, she caught her breath.

"Tell me if it's too much," the masseur said, and put his elbow into my back, leaned his weight into it.

"Everything," Mama said. "Everything."

Then, while I lay there in the fiery spasm summoned by one who knows its ways and channels and frequencies, my mother went on to tell her masseur the whole shebang, how her daddy'd cut his leg off in a wood cutting accident and got hooked afterward on morphine and she'd have to massage phantom charley horses from the stump, how he'd flown off to Boston to get fitted for a prosthetic and the family'd fallen to pieces, how she was in Sarah Fountain's home room

English class at Central High School in Little Rock, Arkansas on the day they integrated and Governor Faubus had called in the national guard to keep it from happening and ten thousand Arkansans had stood in the streets before the school screaming, *Go Home, Nigger, Go Home*, and she knew she'd have to get out or die, and she'd met Buddy Washer at the Air Force base one fall day when the light was Jack o'lantern orange on the river and he'd known that the effect was called *seiche*, when light did that on water, and she'd fallen in love with the word, how he'd thrown it out easy as pie—she'd fallen for Buddy Washer with his movie star smile and perfect teeth, the relatives he had in the Arizona State Legislature, and the ancestral farm where great, great grandmother Katy'd danced with Geronimo in a field of blue sage and rabbit brush, how Vi could see me inside her, sniff that she was about to run, how Buddy'd hidden outside in the bushes during a thunderstorm and come one inch from taking her blue-eyed baby boy and doing who knows what to him, so that O.W.'d come into the picture because nobody'd ever fuck with him in a million years, he was *that* bad, flat-topped truck driver who'd thrown a ninety-five-mile-an-hour fastball for the scouts, only they'd wanted him to play outfield and he'd said *fuck that*, drove a bread truck, that's how they met, so Buddy never did show up again, not after the pea picking years at Tucker Prison Farm, only O.W. himself was a danger she hadn't thought through, he was a thousand miles from *seiche*, she'd given him a son, Jimmy, but the boozing and whoring and fighting took him away from her, three times married and divorced, how they'd split each other's skulls open, him hauling off and burning her wedding dress in a fifty-five gallon drum out by the well house, he'd got mean on her, nasty, but they'd got Jesus—hadn't they?— and O.W. put the bottle down, if not the gloves, and then Jimmy, nineteen and sawdust bronze, his whole life shining golden before him, how one night he'd said, "Mama, I'll see you when I get home," only he never came home, it was a State Trooper knocked on the door at 4 a.m., Jimmy's wallet in his hand, his face smiling up at her from the man's hand, *I'm sorry, Miss, I'm so sorry, I'm so, so sorry,* and they'd laid him down at Solgahatchia in the Stepwell Bottoms, in May when the fields shone with brown-eyed Susan, and she thought she would die.

"*Oh my,*" the masseur kept saying. "*Oh my.*"

After, we dressed, drove home. Renee and baby Lara were in the tiny bathing pool filled with silver water. Mother and child with smiles like Christmas, and across the street a moving van—the newlyweds had arrived. The bride waved at us shyly from the front porch, disappeared through the screen door.

Mama smelled like eucalyptus, wrapped in dark glasses. "That was me once," she said.

I hadn't thought about it for a long time, our massage, how that last time she'd visited Mama'd said *everything hurt.* There was a house on Camilla Street in Tucson, Arizona, where Mama and my blood father'd first lived after they'd run from Arkansas to the Wild West. I learned to walk in a house like the one across my street, when she was twenty, a girl, Lara's age today. At night time, before she left him there and the Greyhound bus to Arkansas, she'd lay in bed, the sad light would fall from a streetlight with a busted globe, and she'd plan the new life where my father simply did not exist. Snow would fall on the Catalina Mountains, so mid-mountain cactus would bloom fierce and alive, hard to look at by the light of day.

7. Buddy Washer

Them football pictures Josie sent, the ones where you was kneeling in red and white with that brand new football between your white cleats, I had half the boys at Charro's believing that my flesh and blood son was starting tailback for Texas A & M. Believe 'at shit? She sent the articles too, cutouts from the *Democrat-Gazette* about how you'd run for two-hundred-seventy-five yards against Bauxite Pirates, scored six touchdowns and led the state in rushing for ten weeks in a row—how on earth do you stretch that, it was like you were doing in real life what I'd never even thought to make up. Hell, you were ten goddamn feet tall. We had 'em going. We was on a roll. And they could see me in you, the boys at Charro's, and they'd go me a round or two for siring you, and Mama Vi, she could see me in your face, your nose, she said, and my daddy too—I never met him. How's your teeth? I got my teeth from Daddy. Your daughter, her teeth? Say son.

So when the graduation invite come we had a family meeting out at Katy's. Katy's your great grandma on Mom's side. She lived down in Tombstone and her daddy was Johnny Tremaine who was sheriff, put all them gunslingers under Boothill, look it up in the goddamn encyclopedia, I shit you not. Anyway, Josie sent me that graduation invite for May 9, 1979, and Mom called a family meeting so we all drove down to Katy's outside Tombstone—I brought the goat, we grilled her in a hole over charcoal. You cook? Josie was godawful—could burn water. If it was possible, she'd burn it. I mean, what did you eat all that time growing up? Beans? Did she raise you on pinto beans and ketchup sandwiches? Hear? So we grilled the goat down at Katy's and Mom laid a spread on this spot we always went to for family meets, in the grass out under the Geronimo tree, this big ass cottonwood he slept under sometimes when the army was after his ass, cause he ran from them all the time, just take a band of starved elders and squaws and haul ass down into Mexico, hide out in arroyos and cactus, steal some cows, the stray dog or two, live under rocks. It wasn't his real name, Geronimo. That's the name the army boys give him because when he jumped out from under a rock with a knife between his teeth they'd shit their pants and scream SAINT GEROME, who knows what his real name was. He was Chiricahua, and they bury their afterbirth under a tree, and that becomes the center of the child's world—his *omphalos*. 'At's a big ass word, huh? I taught it to Josie. And some other ones. Just means center, your North Star, something like that.

Anyway, we grilled this hillbilly-goat and ate it under the Geronimo tree. Your Mama tell you we buried your sack there, under the Geronimo tree? No? Well we did, and it's there still, that's your center, the center of your universe, if you buy that Apache load. Why you think you keep coming back?

So what I'm saying is we had our meet under that tree and ate our dog named goat, we named all our dogs goat then, except the ones we named pig.

Mom said, "Show us what you brung."

It was all quiet under the tree when she said that. The breeze rustled the cottonwood leaves, that's where Katy's ghost lives, up in those branches, hiding with Geronimo. She'd brought him a cantaloupe. He showed her the knife he'd skinned a white girl with, let her touch the pouch made from its skin. It was soft, she said, like a baby.

So I took it out, the invite, and it got passed up to Andy's end—he's my big bro, Uncle Andy, then down to Davey, you know him, he's little bro, Dirty Davey he goes by.

Mom said, "Buddy boy?"

I said, "Yeah, Ma."

"What's your plan?"

Have I told you about the sky, the color blue of your eyes and mine, your mama used to say, same color when the sun shine on them, she wanted them to be brown like hers, but they come out blue like me, Katy's blue. The sky was that color blue, March, monsoon time when the desert blooms like a house on fire. Like a slit throat. You know?

"Go." Andy said. "It's the right thing. Now's time." He took off his hat, your Uncle Andrew. He took out his wallet and pulled some greeners, stuck them in and passed her own. It was the best goat I ever cooked, that day under the G tree.

There was two, three hundred some dollars Ma dumped on my plate when all was done. "Take this. Make things right," she said, gave me that look, the one that meant she'd cut your nuts off if you broke your word. She's like that, Ma.

I said, "I will."

Davey said, "I'm not going this time."

I said, "Don't blame you little bro."

Uncle Andy asked for his hat back, Ma went to the house for pie, and it was done. Made the phone call to your mama, and she said it was okay, that I could bring the money as a gift from the family, and we could meet and she wouldn't call the police or sic that man of hers on me, and that we could have some time together, you and me.

"What does Dee think about this?" I asked her at the tail end, but we got cut off that second, the party line went dead. Listen to me. *Dead.* Happened all the time. Goddamn hillbilly party lines.

'At last part was a lie.

They never give me no money.

I have obligations. There's my job. I'm a ground electrician. Did I tell you I was in electric?

And if a man understands electric, he knows about everything there is to know, put that in your pipe and smoke it. I bet you don't even know what electric is, I mean, if you had to explain it to a alien, what'd you say? About electric? Looky here, ain't nobody I ever met in my life answers 'at one right.

Give her a shot? Say?

> The study of electricity today comprehends a vast range of phenomena, in all of which we are brought back ultimately to the fundamental conceptions of electric charge and of electric and magnetic fields. These conceptions are at present, not explained in terms of others. In the past there have been various attempts to explain them in terms of electric fluids and aethers having the properties of material bodies known to us by the study of mechanics. Today, however, we find that the phenomena of electricity cannot be so explained, and the tendency is to explain all other phenomena in terms of electricity, taken as a fundamental thing.
>
> The question, "What is electricity?" is therefore essentially unanswerable, if by it is sought an explanation of the nature of electricity in terms of material bodies.

That's the *Encyclopedia Goddamn Britannica.* So I tricked you. Sorry. 'At one's got me many a brewski at Charro's cause they ain't no answer. Anything you say's wrong. Nobody can tell you what it is, and it's everywhere, in your body, even, in your cells, your atoms, the particles of your atoms. Believe 'at shit? I seen it blow a man's boots off one time. We was stringing wire over to Mount Mitchell outside Clifton, me and Todos Martinez, *Toady*, we called him. He was up in the bucket and I was uncoiling wire up the pole, it smelled like creosote, you ever smell creosote? it's oily like gasoline and has this kerosene taste that gets under your tongue so you can't spit it out, but bread helps. So me and Toady, we're munching down on Wonder Bread that day, it was Monday, it was Mayday, and we was hanging wire on the May Pole up on that mountain breathing creosote and munching white bread, Toady singing his little Toad song in Spanish. He had a boy named Toady 2, and he was singing *Toady 2, I love you*, only in Spanish which was pretty good sounding that Monday, which I've always felt bad about—who wants to die on a Monday? Shitty way to start your week.

He took a glove off, I don't know why. His shoes, both of them, they was smoking when they hit the ground. I remember the soles, the hex in the tread, smoke rising. He was cooked, Toady. Somebody'd have to tell his boy that thirty thousand watts of the pure stuff had passed through his daddy's flesh and blood. He'd have to grow up picturing that, how it must've been for his daddy. I thought that of a sudden when I smelled him, just before the bucket fell, knocked me down with him, so we both lay there, and the smoke got in my eyes, it was Monday and I was sorry.

I'm sorry I missed your graduation day. I'd of given the world to be there, you know that.

In your heart, you know. Tell me you don't know.

How I love you.

Your mama tell you I was in an orphanage? I'll take you there sometime. There's these nuns that carry kite sticks and they'll whip the Jesus out of you in a split second if you look at them sideways, make you stick your arm out and *bam*, this little white line zinging through your brain, *tic-tac-toed* if they hit you more than once. A bell rang out every hour on the hour. I never met my daddy. Mama Vi wounded herself over him. We all got farmed out. In the afternoon the sun threw the Saguaro's shadow thirty feet, its arms bent like an old man's, my daddy's I'd think, and the meanness would come on me, the nuns would slap an *x* over my *o* and the cat won every game, hell with it. That was the story worked best after fights with your mother. Her mama'd divorced that old man Si, got a restraining order on him, and that kind of broke her, she was looking for me and didn't know it when we met. We got married in Texas, got this blind justice up out of bed and said our vows, hauled ass off into the night with the radio playing some Elvis Presley, and we was happy, me and your mama.

She left before I could tell her the other part of the orphanage story, how Mama Vi got well and came for me, and I told those goddamn nuns to kiss my red ass, that would have made it up for her, she'd have stayed if I told her that part.

I'll take you there. One of them had a glass eye, the nuns. She hit me with a stick, said I was dirty inside. When you come see me, I'll show you. It's out by the airport, close to the mission, San Xavier for all them poor Indian kids. I'll show you.

And that cottonwood tree where your afterbirth's buried, we'll go there too. I'll show you that, too. We'll dig it up.

She called once, Josie, when you-ins was on a bus at the station in downtown Tucson, on your way to Disneyland.

"Hello," she said, "It's me."

"Been a while."

"Yeah."

"Joey boy with you?"

'71 or '72. I ain't no historian, Mr. Professor, but it was around then, so you was eleven or twelve, on your way to see Snow White and the Seven Dwarves.

"Um hum. And little Jimmy. He's four now."

"You got two now. One of 'em's mine, you know. You need some money? I got money." I thought about coming and getting you then. Bring Andy and Davey, they both WWF wrestlers. Andy had the belt for a while. Hellfire, we'd of had you home in no time, cooked you a goat, and your Uncle Davey's better than any of them goddamn fake dwarves working union out of Orange County. He was in a movie once. I mean they paid him money to act like a dwarf. Didn't have to say nothing. Kiss my ass. Just stand there and be a dwarf. He got paid for that. Some's got all the luck.

"No," your mama said. "We're about to pull out."

"You could have called ahead. I'd of been there waiting."

"Um hum."

"Will you give him a hug for me. Will you tell him his daddy misses him and wants you to give him a hug?"

"Can do."

That's when I heard your voice, the second time I ever heard you say a word. What was it you said? Say. Remember. "Can you put him on the phone and let me talk to him?"

That's when it went dead. I sat there listening to the dial tone and I thought about stuff, about Toady getting his shoes blown off, about picking peas at Tucker, of how close I'd come to you at the window that night. This lady come on the phone, said please hang up. I asked her to talk to me, to tell me why, to ask for forgiveness.

It was *Jimmy*, you said was with you. His son. Baby brother.

Chickens come home to roost—that's what I said on the phone that night when you told me about his car wreck, your brother Jimmy's, how he went through a windshield and you flew down from DC, had to go out to the wrecking yard and stick your hand in the floorboards that were wrist deep with his blood, how you found his senior ring and took it home to poor Josie, how it killed her, losing her son. And don't get me wrong, I understand how it sounds and why you got so mad and all, but they weren't killing words, no need to fight. When you come see me, we'll make that up. And you got a daughter, I'll meet her someday too—who does she look like most, me? Or her. Chickens come home to roost, oh they do. And you better believe she thought of that too, your mama. Truth is, she took you from me. Without saying goodbye or letting me tell her why exactly I had to go to Nogales some weeks, or make it up to her. She just left. People don't do that, just leave. Not give a man another chance. Say. Take a man's son and give him to another? Payback's hell. That's what I always say.

Besides, you got another bro. Like I told you, his name's Roberto, lives in Vegas, deals cards over there, missing the second finger on his right hand, lost it to a lawn mower when he was eleven. Believe 'at? A *lawn mower*. And we don't even have grass down here—well, except for the rich shits. He's half Mexican and half me— you want his number? He can be your brother now.

I keep those pictures in a shoebox all to itself. She sent all your school pictures. She combed your hair like mine. I caught Roberto looking at them one time, asked *who's that boy? who is he?* and I kicked his ass, put it to him. Fuck with my pictures.

So I had another family, people do it all the time. Roberto's mama's name, Socorro—that name means to scorch, to set on fire—Josie found out about all that, but she never let on, she was too smart for that. When you're in prison, let me tell you something about being in prison. The worst part, the very worst part is when your days are up and you know you'll walk free soon and every second there's a chance something will fuck up, somebody'll say something and you'll say something back, and he'll take a swing and you'll swing back, and before you know it you're in lock down hole on bread and water, and they done tacked on six more months. Every minute closer to getting out is worse until the time is at hand, and the man looks you in the face, and you can tell what he's thinking, that he can sink your ship any goddamn second he wants, but he doesn't, lets you walk, and all on this earth you can think about, the only thought in your head, is to get the hell out of Arkansas and never ever ever go back for nothing. No way. Uh huh.

The night before my flight—the night before you graduated high school, and my people'd put together the medicine bundle of money and that letter, and a picture of us all together—my wife come to me and asked me not to go. It was a trap, she said. They'd put me back in the big house. In the hole. She said, Socorro did, that my real son wore shoes with holes in the soles, that we lived on pinto beans, that she hadn't worn a new dress since we married, that our daughter had a cavity in a permanent molar and that she'd lose that tooth forever soon, and weren't my flesh and blood daughter's teeth as good as a son I'd never even known? She said other stuff. How Josephine had no right to send me that invite, like that would make up for all the years, like the theft of you could be paid back. There's no negative without a positive—the two are the same thing sometimes. Electric'll teach you that, how one thing flows into and from another, and if you ain't careful she'll blow the shoes right off your feet.

So I fixed my girl's teeth. I bought Socorro a new dress, shoes for the boy. And I let it go. I'm sorry, Joey. From where I am now, there's not much to be done about it. But just remember, you got this whole family you ain't ever even seen, and we got this huge spread down in Tremaine County south of Tombstone, and there's horses and cows and sheep—we got this llama looks after the sheep, protects them from coyotes that yip yap at night when the stars come spinning out of control so you can see the Milky Way's bands, the aurora borealis in spring and fall, and I'll teach you to make mutton stew the way the Chiricahua did with sheep. They stole Katie's sheep for slaughter, cooked it up in clay pots, one last feast before the run.

Chickens come home to roost. You live in Utah. Utah touches Arizona. I ain't wanted there. You live on a street near that college. Your wife has blonde hair. Your daughter's eyes are hazel. She goes to a school named Cow Jumped Over the Moon. Her playground has a fence with two gates. One of them locks. The other doesn't.

8. Lara

So, I was a pretend Mormon. I faked it so hard I almost believed I was LDS, which Daddy called LSD, some kind of hippy drug that made you talk to Jesus. I submitted to the will of a higher power, and did not dance within arm's length of the dorks at stadium night for ward number six. In Salt Lake City, there are girls named Gabby Jensen, a cheerleader with hair so blonde it hurt to look at, and the only way to get anywhere near her and her court entourage of snoot-noses in the East High lunch room, where the preps separated themselves from the druggies and the goths and the hippies and straight edgers and general losers like me, was to be MoMo and go to seminary and collectively look down your nose at the gentile filth. I faked wearing garments, Jesus jammies they called them, said I'd been baptized and went to church on Sunday and just couldn't wait for the day when my secret name was whispered into the ear of Eli Newell, and we'd have a ginormous wedding and get sodomized at the Temple. I feigned belief in the Nephites, the Danites, the doctrine of blood atonement and baptism of the dead, the carnal ceremony of sister wives, to subordinate myself to a king husband for all time and space on our own planet—the whole nine yards. She found me out, of course, Gabby. And that was that. At lunch in that room where the dance scene from High School Musical was filmed, where tourists were all the time wandering around asking for Gabby Jensen's autograph because she was surely Sharpay and Eli was Ryan and all the ditsy hair curling and garment-wearing world would never make me one of them. They laughed at me. One day somebody duct-taped the bathroom door shut with me inside and wrote CORRUPT on it in pink magic marker. And that was that. You know that song, "At Seventeen"?—that was me, beauty queens with clear-skin-smiles and homely girls like me. I can't wait to get out of here, put this place in my rearview mirror and drive.

And as long as we're having this talk, for as long as you're listening, remember that time you ordered the prom corsage for me and I was going with Rita Watchtower, and you went to pick the thing up, and the address was Larson Mortuary, and a man in a suit and tie said, "It's absolutely stifling in here," and you followed him past a roomful of display caskets to the floral shop where my corsage lay in a plastic box—remember? And you couldn't get that thought out of your head, the roomful of caskets, the plastic box, the tiny roses twisted into the wristband. You wrote me that letter, I've kept them all. Buying a gift for your only daughter at a mortuary, it reminded you of something, you never said exactly, but it had something to do with the Arizona people, the dwarf and warlock, the daddy you never met. What did it mean Daddy? Why did you throw my corsage away?

Driving to Arizona was Jack's idea.

We'd attended preschool together, me and Jack, Cow Jumped Over the Moon, where the food pantry smelled like fresh baked bread on Wednesdays and the light through the stained glass windows splashed down on our faces and turned us into monsters. There was a playground outside, with this huge tunnel slide and a gate where this man talked to us once until Sister Bodil called the cops on him and he ran away. But this man, he talked to us like he knew us, like he was our grandfather or something, and for some reason I knew him, and he knew my name and birthday and that we'd lived in Arkansas once on a farm in the Ozarks where a man bit daddy's finger off. He knew about MaMa, what had happened to her in her hot tub, and he knew about Uncle Jimmy and he asked me if Mom Dee was dead yet—and he called her witch. He asked me and Jack, did we want ice cream after school, would we like to go to the circus and hang with real dwarves, had we ever seen the Painted Desert or a sixty foot Saguaro? Had we heard of Geronimo?

Then Bodil yelled at him and cell phoned the police, and this grandfather man I somehow knew, he ran around a building and we never saw him again. He'd said, "Don't tell anyone what we talked about. The two of you, I'm your secret."

And then, there was Jack in the East High lunch room, just about the time when Gabby Sharpay found out I wasn't Mormon, and all the preps turned up their noses, and somebody locked me in the bathroom and wrote that word in pink magic marker, it was just about that time when up showed Jack, in the cafeteria on a day when I was eating alone and feeling sorry for myself and ready to quit it all, lie about my age and join the Air Force and learn to fly a fighter jet, fly to the top of the earth's atmosphere and get dizzy, point the nose toward East High School ten miles below and let fly, blow it away.

"Can I sit here," he said.

"I'm not Mormon."

He said, "I'm not either. Mormon."

I said, "Why not."

"Tony Stott says yes."

In Jack's lunch box, one of those blue freezer blocks just like Mom used in mine. A sandwich. Doritos, an apple cored and sliced in two, a Juicy. "Want to split that apple?"

It's funny how people look at you from across the room, then pretend they're not looking when you see them. Daddy has this whole spiel about another sense, about how homo sapiens have evolved this ability to know when they're being looked at—stare out a window at somebody and they wheel around, look you in the face. Feel the hair on the back of your neck stand up, turn around, there's blonde-blonde Gabby Jensen glaring from on high.

"Do we know each other?" Jack asked.

"Who's Tony Stott?" A Polynesian friend was staring now, and Meka Sanchez whose *quinceañera* I'd attended and danced with a boy close enough to smell his b.o.

Jack was sawing the apple into quarters with a plastic knife. "A kid from Kaysville. That's south." Lunch was only twenty minutes or something like that, who eats in twenty minutes? The Korean chicken that day was to die for, I remember, the sesame seeds were toasted, they'd got the sauce just right.

"He's a stoner. Go out and get whacked on weed then show up at this church where they'd baptize him forty times or something for dead people."

A bell was ringing, a buzzer, everybody started moving at once. Outside, through the big open plate glass, a custodian mowed the softball field, little squares into little squares.

"That's too weird."

"I'm Jack. The not Mormon."

I remembered that second that he had been a whistler, that he could pucker and make real song, like that carnival tune or the theme from *Bridge on the River Kwai* or "Somewhere Over the Rainbow." How a man I recognized but didn't know had given us a secret to share, and I'd never told a soul.

"Lara," I said. "From Cow Jumped Over the Moon." I held a hand out. My left one, ringless, clear nail polish, plain Jane.

Everyone was gone now, second bell about to go off so I'd be late to Mr. Tiny's Chemistry lab, and he'd give me zero for the day without blinking an eye, record it while I watched. Smile at me. Peckerhead Mormon.

He said, "I thought that was you. But people change."

That January, the day after my eighteenth birthday, it snowed a hundred and eighteen inches in one day at Alta Mountain, and it was a Saturday, we drove through the tunnel the plows had made, the sun came out, and this golden pixie dust came flittering down so we passed through it, Jack and me. On the first lift the howitzers fired, those anti-aircraft cannons the resort used to blast would be avalanches off the mountainside. *Vroom, Vroom*—weak layers slid into powder rivers roaring. It was the month I was accepted to the University of Utah, the very day, though I wouldn't know till I got home, Daddy cooking chili to celebrate. See, Arkies make chili when it snows, fire up four wheel drives and go off pulling the stranded out of ditches, car wrecks perpetrated by people who were themselves on their way to buy chili fixings, Velveeta for cheese dip. I'd wanted Washington State, or back east, anywhere at all save Utah, but no go, my fate was to live in a deluxe dorm room up on the hill two hundred yards from Old Post Theater where I'd started my period at soccer camp when I was twelve, and the whole mess had come on me while I was waiting to be assigned to group blue or group yellow, but of course it was group red, and Uncle Fred came on me, and it was a shock. I told Daddy I was sorry, I was sorry for growing up.

The top of the lift unloaded right or left, either side calf deep powder, the sun on the far mountains pink and gold, alpenglow. Jack was a woods skier, he liked the deep trails off in shadow, zinging off with me behind, on a Saturday after I'd turned eighteen. Halfway through the first run—was it Molly's Gulch?—I clipped a tip and crashed into a house-high drift, so I was under and it was dark, the snow over my head, and the air disappeared. I don't know how long I lay like that, under the snow. I thought I might just stay there, cozy, alone. I could just go to sleep and escape Utah and its Mormons with their Funeral Potatoes and Jell-O and "Oh my heck" would cease and desist. I didn't know I'd been accepted to the University of Utah, or that Jack had too, and it didn't matter.

"You okay?"

"*Jack.*"

The snow smelt like pine trees and that clean smell when you step outside barefoot as Daddy's people do, Mom too, and run a heart into your backyard on first snow day. "I'm in here. I can't see."

"Yeah."

"Why'd you go so fast? Are you an idiot?"

Snow had got down my pants. I could feel it down there, a cold hand. Light, the sun was out, it was a powder day, we were on the mountain.

"I'm digging," Jack said.

"Hurry."

"Stop talking."

After he got me out, we flew down the rest of the way to Alf's for hot chocolate and foot warming, a whole throng of people from Chicago and New Jersey and L.A., not one person of color among them.

"We should go to Arizona. Just drive on down," Jack said.

We'd already gone through our first free refill and were about to get another, warm now, sleepy almost. Jack wasn't so bad. Daddy'd met him, we'd gone to Cow Jumped Over the Moon together, shared the secret of the man who'd known us all those years back.

"What are you talking about. Why do you say that?" Arizona.

Out the picture window, wind blew a knurl of powder off Mount Baldy's shark tooth peak, a stream whipping south. The eighty-year-old club had three tables, old men guzzling mugs of frosty beer. I'd learned to ski here—*the greatest snow on earth.*

Jack said, "There's saguaros. Sixty footers. The Grand Canyon. The Painted Desert. We could be there tomorrow."

"Do you remember the man?"

His boots were off, Jack's. He said, "Do you?"

"That's what he said. The Painted Desert."

"Our secret."

"Why?"

It was time for a second run, a clean line down the real mountain, out of the woods and into the light. "Why not?"

I said, "You're crazy."

"Good crazy," Jack said.

It was what Grandmother Josie used to say—I knew this because Daddy'd kept her alive for me, said you always carry in your heart the ones that you love. Maybe it was a good sign, Jack knowing to say that.

Good crazy.

9. Buddy Washer

They're thieves, the Apaches, you know? No, really, that's how they made a living as a tribe, make these runs down into old Mexico and steal cows, horses, goats and chickens, a little light-skinned Mexican girl sometimes, bring 'em back and divide up. That's why the Feds had such a time breaking them—I mean—how do you force criminals by nature to abide by a law written by a race who believes in heaven and hell, fire and brimstone, worms and boils for all time, how do you buffalo a people whose mission was to live, take, consume, and die. They had this whole religion based on revenge, so when those soldiers massacred Geronimo's first wife and children, a little girl with his mama's eyes who'd just learned to say whatever Chiricahua word means *daddy*, scalped her and had the squaw before lifting her hair too, when they did that and Old Geronny came home from a thieving raid to find it, he swore hisself an oath in Apache, cut off a hunk of his flesh and buried it there with them, went on the warpath with the white eye. Only his way, his peoples' way, was to hide behind a rock, a tree, three blades of saw grass with a knife blade between the teeth, to make nary a sound nor tremble nor any sign for the senses to grab hold of save that one that knows when its being looked at—you got that one, Joe?—spin around and they's somebody eyeing you from a high place? or the other way, somebody spin around see your eyes looking down on their pitiful ass?—and in a spiffy, slip in and do the deed, be gone before the heart quits beating. Hells bells, sometimes they'd cut it out of the chest, light-foot it back to the rock they'd watched from, take a big ole bite out of it, so they tasted the living person at the moment they died. How 'bout them apples?

'Twasn't his real name, Geronimo.

You see, them soldiers he swore revenge on, they was Mexicans, who'd killed his slender young wife after raping her in her own blood, his three kiddos, and his mama, even, they done her, too. Alope was her name, the squaw, and the man who called himself Goyaalé—the one who yawns—he took his knife out and hacked off all his hair, started walking. Why he walked and he walked and he walked and then he ran, nowheres in particular. And somewhere out there not so far from where great grandma Katy lived, out there with the Gila monsters and saguaro and pink rattlesnakes, this voice come to him, said *no gun will ever kill you. Buddy, you the boss. You got the monkey paw, the mojo, the hot hand. Now get out of here.*

His wife was dead, his kids were dead, they'd scalped Mama. His life was a big fat zero.

Why not just kill ever'body? Say. What would you do?

So he gets permission from the big chief, Cochise, for revenge, tricked the Mexicans into an ambush where he ran willy-nilly this way and that, their bullets turning into water, into rain with the blood red sun out, and he killed them one after another, and when he was out of bullets, he took to slashing them with his knife, and them Mexicans, they'd never seen anything like that before, a spirit warrior who could not be shot, who came out of thin air to slit their throats, a hundred dead or dying, and they started screaming *San Jerome, San Jerome*, and they ran from the place of death screaming the word until it echoed in every canyon. That's how our boy got his name, Geronimo.

For a long time I thought to burn your house down. Take revenge. Cut my hair off and start walking.

But I didn't.

You heard me. 'Twasn't me. No way, José.

And it's not my fault that your mother made that phone call when you was twelve, en route to Disneyland out in sunny California, and the Greyhound stopped over in Tucson and she looked me up and called, then didn't even wait for me to come say hello, kiss my ass, anything at all. I mean, what kind is it calls says my son's right here in the town he was born in, then doesn't even wait for its daddy to come say hi? I was pissed. And I might've thought about it, but it wasn't me burned your house down. Not me, man.

The wood frame house, the one with the two barns and chicken coop, that big Paint named Rebel in the back pasture, those donkeys—Dee's idea no doubt, the cross of Jesus tattooed on their backs—why its wiring must'a been six hundred years old. You and your brother's rooms were on the second floor where all those sisters lived once, and one of them had died so the place was haunted from the get-go, and your loco Uncle Earl had whopped the previous tenant in the head with the butt of a pistol for wanting to take the water heater he'd bought with his own good money. Imagine that, whopping a man in the head for taking what's his. Some people are crazy like that. I'm sure you know some.

Anyways, I don't know why I'm telling you all this. It's what me and Roberto do, shoot the shit. He's your brother, he's missing a finger, and no he's not a dwarf.

He was a drinker, boy oh boy, that new daddy of yourn. And with you and your brother and sister off at the magic kingdom, why I bet he had hisself a good old time and was dead-ass pass out drunk sawing logs when it all went down, when the wires burnt through their tubing, that ceiling sparking to beat the band. About to fall down on him any second, that one ember burning into the heart side of his chest.

He got out in his underwear, hopping one foot to the other. I don't know how I know all this, come to me in a dream, the monkey paw mojo, ain't no gun ever gonna kill me. *San Jerome, San Jerome.*

Wasn't me burned your house down. I'm swearing to God. I've done all sorts of things, but I never done that. It was a coincidence. You've got to know that. And it hurt nary a hair on your head.

But I thought about it. Old Geronny, he walked the revenge trail and it cost him plenty.

Story goes that there at the end, after he'd strangled his own dogs so they wouldn't bark and give away his final escape from the rez, the ragged warrior who could see the future and stop time, who could never be killed by bullets, led a band of thirty-eight, elderly and infirm and generally afflicted, out into the night. They ran—eighty miles in a day sometimes across the desert toward old Mexico, chased by five thousand American soldiers and as many Mexican, throw in a couple hundred bounty hungers who could get $25 for a child's scalp, $50 for a squaw, and $100 for a warrior. Two weeks later at a place called Silver City, they found this girl who'd been taken alive, hung from a meat hook and skinned. The meat hook was jammed into the base of her skull.

She was skinned head to toe.

Surely he carried the skin of that white girl when they gathered out under the big cottonwood where Katy's daddy saw them. The kids climbed up the fire place, hid there, only Katy got out somehow, she walked outside just at nightfall. She picked a cantaloupe from the garden and carried it to these starving, barefoot Apache, the last thirty-nine free Indians alive.

He'd taken the revenge path, Geronimo. Much later he'd sign his name at the World's Fair for a nickel, fake calf roping in a Wild West show, he'd get baptized as a Christian and join the Reformed Dutch Church. He'd lead Theodore Roosevelt's Inauguration Parade and dine with the president and first lady. He'd remember that cantaloupe, how he'd surrendered his gun, his knife in Skeleton Canyon that very week, and the whole sorry lot of them got hauled off to Florida as prisoners of war.

Mercy me—that's what being nice got him, carted off to a goddamn Florida prison like a dog.

Maybe he should have told Katy to go get the rest of the kids, pick a few more of those pink-fleshed melons, they'd all have a good old time out under the cottonwood tree. What I'm saying, see what making nice got him? See?

It's a family story. Your mama liked it.

Teach you a trick. So remember, I'm in the business of being a ground electrician. What that means is that I walk around peoples' houses taking care of their lines and hookups, internal and external outlets, the boxes, installing 220 for new clothes dryers and stoves, stripping out the tube and wire shit from the forties that'll fry your house straight to the ground, running the good stuff up through the ceiling joists which is most often where trouble starts, those hot lines scorching bare insulation, go off like a bottle rocket if you don't watch out. People are stupid. Once I got called to inspect a suspected arson, this goofball who had an old-style fuse box, and instead of fuses he'd stuck pennies in the holes and his place'd gone up with him and his dog. What I'm saying, don't put pennies in your fuse box, don't play with fire, you know that.

Anyway, the trick. So say you drive from the Arizona line to Salt Lake City, take you six hours and change, no problemo. And you got your tool belt with you, couple rolls of wire, your union card and license. Drive into town, see the gold blowhard on top of the Temple, spit on a sidewalk. Walk on into Rocky Mountain Power that away, with your belt on, and say you'd like to report an outage and check the current status for a customer.

"Name," the ditsy clerk will say.

And you say, "Harvell, Joey. 801.273.6525. Near the University."

"159 Hill Street?"

"Zactly."

She's not fond of ground electricians, and that's good cause she wants you out quick, smelling like dirt and copper, a little mustard from your baloney sandwich on the side of your mouth.

"I see no current problem. The meter's in back, up beside the bathroom window."

"Tell me somethin' I don't know, sweets."

She'll look you in the eye that way people who think they're better than you have of looking. "Is there anything else?"

"Permit to inspect."

She's got one all ready. Just slaps the address down in old lady cursive, stamps it official, and passes it over. Just like that. Think about it—the places you could go. I mean, the residencies you could enter if you just put your head to it.

Some fun, huh?

I watched you through the window one Christmas morning and hoped you'd see me there—remember—living in the house two numbers down, it was vacant, the heat was on, what gives? I talked to you on the phone from there, you said you'd come visit, drive to Tucson, and we'd cook a goat, invite the whole family—your homecoming. There'd be Roberto and Reina, bro and sis, they've got good hooter, you know, Dave'd be there—I'm thinking you met him once.

Mama Vi, you'd be her knight in shining armor, how she missed you all these years.

You'd argued, remember? right there in front of that twinkling Christmas tree, you and your old lady—her name's Renee? They'd left a coat in the empty house. It had two dollar bills in one pocket. I had me some whiskey. It was Christmas morning, your fortieth birthday. The girl was a doll. Look like my sister, Ginger—you'd like Ginger, she's a hoot. Your front porch had wood stacked on it real nice, you get that from me, wood stacking. Smoke was coming out the fireplace—all warm and cozy family-like in there, only you and your wife were going at it. What for? What on earth? On Christmas, for goodness sake.

You used to look like me in them football pictures. Now you looked like your granddaddy Si with his hawk nose and blue eye. The little girl opened a gift, give you a big hug, then your wife one. I couldn't tell what the gift was, didn't matter, she was the conduit between you two, I could tell, she was the electricity that ended your fight. Y'all had breakfast, played some *Elvis Sings Christmas* music, and I walked on back to the vacant rental where the heat was on, and there was a phone hooked up on the wall, called Socorro, Roberto and Reina and Mom, all the Mexicans making sugar cookies shaped like dwarves for Davey.

Then I called you, wished you a happy birthday and I could hear their voices in the background with that Elvis stuff. You said you'd come to Tucson in springtime when the cactus bloomed and the monsoon rains make the whole place crazy with color and smell and all those things your mama loved when I first brought her here and we were in love and you was the conduit between us. We'd make it, and you'd have a baby brother coming soon, a little earth-eyed sister, I'd buy us a big goddamn house, lay a barbecue pit out back, grill anytime we wanted and the hell with ever'body else.

I said, "I love you, son. You'll come in spring?"

"I will," you said.

"You promise?"

"Should I promise? Does that make it any truer?"

I said, "Promise."

You see, I didn't really know who you were—I couldn't read you all the way through. Most people, they easy as pie. But I was seeing you through dark glass. "Yes," you said. "It's time."

You said, "My brother Jimmy, he died in a car wreck. That killed Mama."

"Your brother's right here, in my house, this second. Sis, too."

"I loved him."

"He don't know you, but he loves you."

"It was my fault."

Somebody was fiddling with the front door—they seen me through the glass. One of them said *who are you*? "Aint none of it your fault."

"I taught him the shortcut home, that curve he missed on 319."

The music had gone to Motown—why the hell you listen to that jig-music? They were coming in the front door, bastards, who did they think they were, breaking in on me on Christmas? "You'll come home, you promise."

"Merry Christmas, Buddy."

"How about Daddy?"

"I call *Daddy* Daddy."

They'd come for something, then they left, called the man, heard his bubble gum machine outside, and I heard it through the telephone receiver too, we both heard it together, the police.

"Promise."

You said, "I swear on what's most holy to me."

That was Christmas 2002. April came and went. The cacti bloomed to beat the band, then May and June. Joey *no aqui*. Hell yeah I was mad when you called, you see I'd believed in you, you given your word, you sniveling little shit. I'd told the whole bunch you was coming, and they believed me. Goddamnit, they *believed* me. You know how hard it is to get family to believe anything at all. So we had it planned, and Mama Vi even made arrangements at the church to make it official, you'd be one of us again, bygod. Ginger sewed you a blue shirt from fabric she bought off the Navajo, they believe blue's luck, she made you a goddamn lucky shirt. Davey knew you'd never come all along, never said a word, little pissant.

What I'm saying, when you called me and said Josephine had drowned, why everybody died, she'd got old, her time had come, my time's coming, yours. Chickens come home to roost. The point was you'd stabbed me in the back. I could have had you forty times, kick that piece of shit door down and take you screaming, but I had to be Mr. Nice Guy, give you a chance, let you make the decision on your own, and look what happened, you stabbed me in the back.

The truth is, you said you'd come. You promised. On what's most holy to you. And I waited.

But I ain't waiting no more.

I've got two sons. A daughter. They're here with me now. You are zero, *nada*. I never should have surrendered, you know. I should have fought those fuckers until I was the last one standing. They never would have took me to prison. Somebody takes your wife, your kid, your life. What else is there but to kill them all?

Adios, hijo.

Los muertos no hablan.

10. Joey

Barely home from Mama's funeral, we'd headed west. I made the call an hour before we hit the road, the number I'd thrown away so many times I knew it by heart. You answered on the third ring. Renee and Lara'd gone off to walk the dog. It was the 12th of July, a Friday, my paternal grandfather Si's 84th birthday, not so hot, the moon new, our spring garden going to seed.

I couldn't get the taste of salt water out of my mouth, like I'd swallowed too much ocean that afternoon of the Florida Blue Run when Mama drowned in Arkansas. A friend said go sympathetic with it, think margarita and french fries, homegrown tomatoes. None of it was right, how it had gone down during Poppy's birthday in Florida, Daddy's call after midnight, the fierce bright casket out under the afternoon sun in Solgahatchia, my mama in there—it was all fucked up, and I was running, I'd go as far as I could, there was danger strewn all behind me, coming at my back, and I knew that the right thing, Buddy, was to talk to you, to tell you that your child bride, your brown-eyed girl from Little Rock that summer of 1959, that she was gone—that she'd *gone home*, O.W.'d said into my ear through a phone cold to the touch. He'd repeat renditions of that midnight phone call more than once over the years, his voice melodramatic, inflicting the news. I, too, would dream of burning his—and in turn my—house down.

We were headed for Oregon, the coast, as far from Arkansas and its First Baptist Church and square-neck preachers who'd hold you under water till you drowned, from the smell of burned flesh sprayed over with Glade and the aroma of hot tub chemicals, we were going as far from all that as we could get, the three of us—Lara, Renee, me.

The dreams had started. Mama talking to me from the dead. *Joey*, she'd say. *Joe? Why don't you love me?* A year later, just as they foreclosed the house on Willy

Ray, the one house Mama ever owned that O.W.'d mortgaged for all it was worth—
you see, they had an insurance policy that paid the house off if either one of them
died—and bought a tri-level on Goathead Golf Course in J-Ville, Trace would say
that she was still in that room, that she'd scared the shit out of her and Dougie, that
they just couldn't take it any more. Is that what the newly dead don't know, but learn?
That we want them to stay dead like they're supposed to, not be calling our names
through the walls of time. And years later, when Renee's mom passed, I'd remember
again, because there she'd be, sitting on the edge of the bed, and Renee'd bolt upright
screaming and the wind would blow through the screen and somewhere a car door'd
open, shut.

"You said you'd come see me."

The house smelled how a house smells when nobody lives in it for a while, when
the air has grown stale inside and all the lunch meats in the refrigerator have gone
rancid. The cherry tomatoes in the wooden bowl on the back porch had split open and
leaked. Fruit flies flew in our mouths when we breathed.

Emphysema rattled in your lungs—I could hear it, the phlegm. I said, "Mama's
dead. She drowned in her hot tub."

Saying it didn't make it any more real—remember this, there's no preparation
ever been conceived for the bewilderment of burying your mother. You didn't know
this, I'll give you that. Vi lived, she had yet to pass.

"You goddamn little liar."

I said, "I wanted you to know. Mama would have wanted me to tell you. She
only spoke about you once. In a thunderstorm. When I was scared. She said you had
good teeth."

"I don't want to hear any of this. I don't care. Got it? You said you was coming
home. We made plans. You goddamn little shit liar."

You raised your voice then, you screamed at me. It was loud coming through the
receiver, and just then Lara walked in, she was four years old—look what she'd been
through, *how now brown cow*, Mama used to say.

I said, "You don't know me well enough to scream at me."

We met eyes, Lara and me, and I could see the question there, and I wouldn't
know that I'd remember this on a day down the road when I'd scream at her, when I'd
say some of the same words that we both heard come from your mouth.

She heard what you said next—there was no way around it. I slammed the phone
into its cradle. A piece of it broke off and skittered across the floor. I knew I'd never
talk to you again. That we'd said our last words.

Sometimes I'd go online, type in incarnations of your name, see if your obituary came up.

That's how I found Vi's, her obit, and learned for the first time the names of my Arizona people, that you were Catholic, my brother's wife and sons' names. A story came up from *The Tucson Times* about Davey being Santa's little helper at a south side Christmas party for the underprivileged. They interviewed him and he talked about his time on the tour with the World Wrestling Federation, how he'd worked as Dirty Davey and Little Lord Fontelbury, what it had been like to travel the world as a wrestling dwarf and how he felt like he owed something back now. He'd been in the movies, Mama'd said, was the big star of the family, and I wished I could find the photo Mom Dee had given me of all those Washer brothers and sisters on the blanket with dwarf Davey holding his arms up like Hercules, Uncle Earl behind him, a cigarette in his mouth. Lara'd been amazed at all that, that she was related by blood to a dwarf, that she could birth a dwarf baby. He'd come to the funeral, Davey, and I remember how I recognized myself in his face, how he'd stood on tiptoe to sign her book, how he said we'd catch up to each other sometime, that he had a lot to pass my way. That he would catch up to Lara, too, he'd called her *cutie*.

A million miles away, all that.

I quit thinking about it. Raising my daughter, season in and season out with Renee, the endless wrappings of the swamp cooler in Octobers while it rained, how spring time came roaring, blizzards when the pussy willow bloomed, grown men mowing their lawns barefoot in May snow, the tails of compost rats making straight lines to the one opening under my built-on study. Mom Dee died in September, and I didn't go home, I'd had it with funerals, always the fake grass laid out beside the grave, so many people picking bits of fried chicken from between their teeth while we sang "Amazing Grace" and "I'll Fly Away," those songs that scathed their ways into the heart. And I laid blocks around all the graves, Jimmy's, Mama's, troweled the grout thin on O.W.'s side. I'd burned sage and watched the smudge whirl up through the hickories with the smell of bitterweed and pond water, the cows bellowing, the horses down on their knees drinking, the redneck shirtless peckerwood smoking on his front porch off in the distance, all of us come down from Henry County, Tennessee, to Solgahatchia and the Trail of Tears to get buried in the hardpack dirt that overlooked a lighting struck tree and a hundred-yard-long chicken house out so far in the country they had to paint fence posts purple which meant *posted* to folk who couldn't read. Let the dead bury the dead. I'd had it with all that.

The last time I saw her, Mama, was the year after we moved back from Moreland Road in Dover. I'd up and quit my job in history at ArkaTech College in the cow pasture, and we'd moved back to our Utah house—thank Jesus it hadn't sold. And Mama'd seen it coming, we'd parted on Mother's Day, she'd cried and couldn't stop crying.

"I'm sorry, Mama" I said.

"You should be."

It had been at Mom Dee's apartment, we'd driven there for Mother's Day and Dee'd made a cherry pie. I brought ribs, and a newspaper with a piece I'd written called "The DeSoto Historical Presence in the Natural State" which talked about him crossing the Arkansas River at flood stage, how big cottonmouth moccasins had latched onto the necks of horses and a whole lot of his hogs had drowned, which I thought was funny, the ancestral breeding stock of the Razorback, swimming the Arkansas with a skinny Spaniard.

Mama was having none of it. We stood out in the grass for a while when it was over, the sun bright on her face, and that's when she started crying, the way her mouth quivered and then Renee had cried, and Dee had tried to cheer us up by getting Lara to say jiggity jig—home again, home again, *jiggity jig*.

I'd hugged her, that smell of White Shoulders and cigarette smoke, and something I never could place, though it reminded me of Jimmy, that olfactory recognition of kith and kin, these were my people, that's what the smell said, and I was leaving them, heading west, taking my family with me. Who'd tend the family cemetery when I was gone, hold Christmas dinner and hide the Easter eggs. Jimmy was gone, it all would have been different if Jimmy hadn't been killed that way. It broke our spirit, Jimmy's car wreck.

Cain, where is thy brudder, the preacher'd said. And then he said it three more times, looking me in the face, so a quiet fell over the congregation and all you could hear were the people who were crying.

That broke us.

I flew home from Utah for her sixtieth—forty, sixty, eighty, that's how it went for me, Mama and Floradee. We threw a party at Trace's house, only her husband—everyone called him Superman because he'd survived six heart attacks at thirty-five—sat on the couch eating popcorn with the TV full blare so we had to sing Happy Birthday over it, and Mama'd blown her candles out and I could see the painkillers in her eyes, there in the double-wide trailer off Mount Carmel road in Lonoke, Arkansas—November, a week from Thanksgiving.

I drove the rental to the house on Willy Ray one last time before heading for Little Rock and the airport and the plane ride home. All of the windows were heavily covered. The light hurt her eyes. It was dark in our living room. None of the family photos were visible in the hallway.

I said, "Mama. It's dark in here."

"I know. Isn't it?"

Over there was the dark space where we'd had our family dinners, her heaping bowlfuls of good spaghetti and garlic bread, deep leafy salad and a shake canister of Parmesan cheese. It was where Daddy'd said his first prayer after walking the aisle at First Baptist and dedicating his heart and life to Christ, so church folk jumped up and shouted as if Satan's own right hand man had turned toward the light and thrown down the sword he'd bloodied on the skulls of the just. James Lonn Spenst had hid us from him in his house one winter, when I'd been asked to play tackle for the eighth grade team whose game had followed our seventh grade match up at Jackrabbit Field, only when it was over there was no Mama to pick me up, and I stood under this big oak tree until a cop picked me up, drove me home to find Daddy drunk in a rage, showed up at the house after a month away, about to kill everybody with the fireplace poker. Jimmy started to stutter then, that very night. Mama sent me out to start the Pontiac, came running with Jimbo, Trace in tow, and I got to drive us out, spew gravel all up our drive. I screamed *son of a bitch, son of a bitch* out the rolled down window into the frosty night, and I could see him back there, running after us, hollering and unintelligible.

The bay window looked out on what used to be an orchard, where these big ass fruit spiders spun webs tree to tree, so if you walked out there at night, say on your way to the barbed wire fence you'd climb through to walk down to the cedar barn where Tauyna Barnett, dance instructor from Milly's House of Tap, sat wrapped in a horse blanket with stripes of moonlight across her flesh, only you walked into one of those ten foot tall webs and it wrapped around your face, and you screamed Jesus Goddamn Christ, and felt it coming, the monster with all eighty eyes intent on your blood.

I said, "I love you."

"I know. I've always known."

"*Bye, Mama.*"

"Bye."

I drove all the way down Willy Ray, hung a left toward Templeton's IGA where Daddy'd killed a deer he'd run over with a tire tool, and I turned around, drove back, walked through the door, and she was on the couch, crying into a blue blanket.

"Why are you crying, Mama?"

She said, "You're so sweet." And that time, when I shut the door behind me, that was the last time I ever saw her alive. I guess we both knew it down deep in that place we shared, the vessel that had born me to birth on her blood. She called me her *soul mate*, not to my face but to her friends, Dora, Floy Melton, that skinny peckerwood from California.

I hit Little Rock, boarded the plane, and saw snow shining on the Wasatch Mountains before noon. That was when I left Arkansas for good—the last time I saw Mama alive.

There's a stiff brown notebook on the right hand side of my desk, in the filing cabinet, in front with my insurance papers and retirement. Inside are my adoption papers, the new birth certificate with my name changed to Harvell. I had to petition the Pima County Court because, you see, they never officially went through with it, my adoption, the name I went under for my whole life, the one I gave Renee and Lara, I was a Washer all along. So my wedding certificate is a sham, my social security card, I was yours all along.

Mama never knew.

She'd already been killed by the time I got it settled, when I became legally a Harvell, O.W.'s name, the name they'll carve on my tombstone, on Renee's in Solgahatchia where they bury my kind. So I'm the one who did that, not Mama, not O.W., and not Dee. I'm the one who went through with it, even though I didn't have to. It was all me. Mother fucker. All me. The chickens come home to roost.

You shouldn't have said that last thing when I called you to say Mama'd drowned. You never should have.

So I was halfway expecting you to call back, out of the blue some day when thunder came and the sun shone bright while a silver rain fell, and a rainbow came out in the same place it always does, to the east, just over Mount Olympus. But you never did call back. And it was a jolt, let me tell you, when I came across it, the obit, *your* obituary:

William "Buddy" Washer

Born August 18, 1937, died September 19, 2005. Buddy served in the U.S. Air Force during the Korean Conflict and Vietnam. Preceded in death by his parents, James and Violet and sisters, Jackie and Eva and son-in-law, Francisco Esquer. Survivors include his wife, Socorro; daughter Reina; sons Roberto and Daniel; sisters, Janet, Ginger, Cita, Sarah and Susan; brothers, Andy and Davey; grandchildren and other family members. Visitation 5-9 p.m. on Thursday with a Rosary at 7 p.m. on Thursday, September 22, 2005. Funeral Mass 10:00 a.m. Friday, September 23, at St. Monica Catholic Church with burial to follow at South Lawn Cemetery.

You died on a Sunday. Lara saw a snake that day in the foothills, sipping from the creek that runs down from the mountainside. Don't ask me why I noted this on the calendars I've kept all these years.

Truth is, I don't know.

Part 2

11. Davey

What's hard is finding pants. I mean, hell's bells, walk into a men's department on the south side, say a place over by the plasma center off Cochise, and this cat with a tape measure around his neck gives me that back alley smile like we're both in on the same joke, says, "You know, bud, our Junior two-for-one sale ended last Satday." Good goddamn luck finding a thirty-eight inch waist with an eighteen inseam hanging on the racks. There are no stores for my kind of people and try paying a seamstress to do a cut down, cost you your balls and then some. Shirts, no problemo, 17 1/2 neck, short sleeves, tuck that baby in deep. Shoes, piece of cake, 6 wides. My head's big as the next guys, so hats aren't a sticking point. First thing the lady's want to know—ev*erything good down there.* A-okay. Belts, underwear, socks, got 'em up the kazoo. A simple pair of say Levis, impossible. Back on circuit we had this woman named Big Velma who did our costumes any way we wanted. Glitter, dye, glow in the dark, you name it, Big Velma had you covered. She sewed me a leather jerkin once with Dirty Davey in silver cursive across the butt, she was an artist, Big Velma. She had a tattoo of an eye between her breasts and she could make it wink or stare or give you the evil eye, I'm swearing. She could do a cut down faster than I can fry eggs, which she loved over homemade biscuits, easy, with a shake of salt and a ground of pepper, a wedge of cheddar on the side. She'd cut and sew the bottom seam, iron steam and starch into the suckers, and I'd fry her eggs sunny side up, so they looked like the eye she'd flash you on the sly. But I'm not on the circuit any more, am I? And sweet Velma's third eye has shut, God bless her. And that niece of mine, she's on her way down from Utah this second, and today's Veteran's Day so the parade's on in South Tucson. Hell's bells, I'm thinking.

That's what Big V always said, *hell's bells,* her red eye winking. Pants, I need new pants.

In Charro's, it's all Trumpet this, Trumpet that, a hundred conversations blaring in the smoke-filled air, the front door wide open, free PBR draft for Vets all the live long day.

November 11, 2016, it's a Friday, and Fridays are different than other days, don't you know. Something hopeful and right about leaning into the weekend at Charro's after election day, when your country's just elected for its president a man whose photograph is very much at home up on Charro's Wall of Fame with the Commancheros, leather vests wide open to hairy chests, Colt and Ronnie Dupree with their arms big as tree limbs, who'd ever guess in a million years they were lovers, meanest tag team ever crawled through the ropes, both of them possessors of sleeper holds that would send you home to Jesus, I'm swearing. There's Haystack Calhoun, six-hundred pounds in overalls, he fell through the ring once, left a hole six feet wide, kept on falling plumb through the basement, broke a water main so all of DeWalt Street flooded for ten days and nights, but God could he tomahawk a ring, take up half the floor, that big-ass country boy smile. Bruno Santini was the first man to ever lift Haystack off his feet in the ring, and look where that got him, a fight with the Sheik who tore his head off.

On a little further is the man hisself, Ace Charro, who the place is named for because he got be an extra in that Elvis movie filmed over at Apache Land Movie Ranch, *Charro With Elvis* it was called, weren't they two peas in a pod. He wore a mask with a big black ace over his face and this poncho with golden threads woven into the fringe that once belonged to Poncho Villa, that's what Serial Killer said, anyways, like you can believe a word out of his mouth. A little further, not entirely to the bathroom, there's The Fabulous Kangaroos and The Great Mephisto, Sheik and The Angel of Sorrow who was famous for biting the heads off live chickens. Me. The Lumberjacks were real life brothers, Rusty and Danny Wallers, they feuded with anybody and everybody, especially the Commancheros, Black Mamba and Bone Crusher. Big Daddy Winslow's team The Grapplers. El Diablo was sometimes cheered, sometimes not—he could swing both ways depending on what was needed on a given night's card. President Elect Trumpet's beside Diablo, those pouty lips and flip-over hairdo just like Jimmy Shins used to wear, get Big Velma to spray a whole can of Paul Mitchell Extra Body Firm on him, man did he ever have a 'do. The framed photograph is signed from the campaign visit: *For All The Boys at Charro's—*

Grab Them By The Pussy. Which strikes me as downright embarrassing about now, waiting for Buddy's granddaughter come walking through the door.

Here's what I know.

Fifty-five years ago, when Buddy drove up with that dark-haired beauty Josephine Stepwell in his serious overheated car, Cochise Street was same old, same old. They'd driven all night, had been married *by a sleepy justice in the big heart of Texas*, how Buddy put it, which turned out to be a lie, after all. She carried his child already, and had come expecting something different than Mama Vi's trailer with roast goat for dinner. They set up shop over on Pima, and brother tried, he tried to be a regular guy and go to work and be an electrician, but he wasn't cut from that cloth, anyone could tell. The smuggling was to keep Socorro and her kids fed over on the Nogales side—he didn't mean anything by it, that's just how it worked—do what you have to do. And he was incarcerated when the boy was born. It was a troublesome birth, that's the blue God's truth. How it happened.

"Hell's Bells, Chopper. Will you fill my glass or do I knock you silly?"

Chopper's afternoon barkeep, everyone pretending they fought at Iwo Jima or Nam or Korea, a whole bevy of Desert Storms, Afghans and Pakis. Everyone's a war hero on free beer for Vet's day.

"What's the occasion?"

From the stool, I'm still looking up at him, that misty patch in his right eye. The Cubbies won. "It's Vet's Day. Our man's in the big house."

"Who'd you steal them new pants off?"

Rod Von Steiger's son walks in with Cat Woman and Stingray, sooner or later everyone darkens the door. "Just fill me, barkeep."

It's cold and salty, the beer.

The Miller High Life clock above the cash register says ten after five. She's late, the Harvell girl. Last time I saw her was at Josie's funeral—fourteen years ago, the Washers had sent me as emissary. I'd shaken the boy's hand—he looked like Buddy, with a smather of his grandpappy Si, and the pissed-offedness in his eyes of his grandma Dee, Lord God, I hope the girl hadn't taken after *her*.

So Josie gets word of Socorro and the Mexican family—people been doing that here for all time, two families separated by the border, legal on either side. Took off for Arkansas without saying bye, who does that with a man's son? It's not how things are done. He talked me into driving out there and there was that business with Pine Bluff Scoggins—what a mess, could've thrown me in the shithouse too, right with Buddy. And people like me don't fare well in the lock down, get the dirtiest jobs, the ones closest to the ground like shoveling out the outhouse, or changing rubber water hoses in the man's pea pasture, shoveling shit out sheriff's horse barn, digging up his dog's business.

We got out, I did, Scoggins, Bud after a year at Tucker. Josie sent pictures of the boy as a football player, and Buddy had everyone in Charro's buying him beers, believing he was tailback for Texas A&M. He could lie the chrome off a trailer hitch, my bro.

It's not like I'm going to know her the second I see her. A lot changes in fourteen years.

And she's a college girl. What's a college girl look like. Especially now, all the field hippy coeds over to U of A marching around with signs saying NOT MY PRESIDENT or BLACK LIVES MATTER or LOVE TRUMPS HATE, or KEEP YOUR LITTLE HANDS OFF MY PUSSY.

You think the Mexicans would know better, causing a stink. Send your ass home to Los Tajitos, just like that. As for me, politics is the big card, makes the rootenest tootenest tag team fuckup gig look tame. And this Trumpet, he's got the chops down, the timing, when to throw the sucker punch, how to end it all with the sleeper. Turn your back on a man like that, wake up in Tijuana, worse. How he horse-hopped Hillary, why she never stood a chance, it was like the White Rider reaching through the ropes to tag Tonto, with Sheik already launched from the top of the far ring, about to crash his spine with elbow and knee. Hippies, who needs 'em. My pants are too tight, they hurt my privates.

Ginger says he talked about the boy on his deathbed. That he'd pleaded with her to call him up in Utah so they could talk one last time and make peace, that he couldn't go into the next world with all that weight hung around his neck, that some way or another it all needed to come clean. It was four years after Josie passed, and Buddy'd picked my brain right and left about the funeral: was that crazy Earl Stepwell there? did Floradee still live? how did she die, again, Josie? Had she hurt? How tall was the boy? Was he Buddy's? Could I see the Washer in him? His child, would she drive south one day? Did she have Vi's grit? That fire in her eyes? Did she favor Ginger in the face?

Problem was, he'd lost the number. Thrown it away, likely.

Ginger tried to get it from information, no go. The university wouldn't give out shit, and the missing persons sham with the state police didn't work neither. His other family was there with him at the end, Socorro with her sweet brown eyes and trembling hands, Roberto, Reina—they were there for his last. But's it's like they say, you remember most the fish you didn't catch, the one that got away.

I've learned to predict the first thing somebody's about to say to me, after they've looked me up and down and smiled or frowned or got nervous, looked at their shoes. There's always this quiet that's pregnant like church. The air gets heavy. Then it gets heavier. It's at these times, when the air's got heavy, that I've learned to hold off, to hold the gaze of whoever's just looked up from their shoes. Hold my tongue. Because what happens next can be turned to my favor, but you got to wait, hold your horses.

So that's what I do when she walks through the front door of *Ace Charro's*, a jolt of sunflower in the eyes she turned the length of the bar until they found mine so that she nodded, and the place went quiet, free beer for Vet's Day in the home of the brave and land of the free where anything on earth could happen now that the future and past lifted glass to the present. We measured each other.

Yes, the silence was like church, like that far off prayer said from the stool at the foot of the wooden man.

She didn't blink, just stood there, about to say. We were on the ropes—the whole gaudy lot.

And until she opened her mouth and said the words, it was as if we awaited news from a world we'd lost, forgot, and suddenly remembered, loved.

12. Lara

So, on a morning like this, with the full snow moon its closest since 1948, the year when my grandmother Josephine was eight and her parents had yet to divorce and she'd never dreamed in a million years that she'd end up in Tucson, Arizona, in the company of dwarves and thieves and dog eaters, what better than rolling the windows full down, the night's dream fresh on my face, the salt lake silvering west toward the Sierra Nevadas and California and the Pacific Ocean, head south, and with every mile draw the great circle of my blood closer to being closed? No, that's not what I'm thinking at all; like her, I have no idea what I move toward, or why.

Poppy and Rose have flown here for early Thanksgiving on Sunday. I'm eighteen. When I look back on this day, from the mountain time makes, will I be able to say why? What force has driven me to take Mom's Subaru, pack credit cards and Fritos and a mummy bag, hit the road past Mormon towns named Goshen and Mona and Nephi, one white steeple glowing whiter than the last, Angel Moroni blowing east on top of each. The speed limit's eighty and I'm flying, old Neil choiring me onward— singing of rivers and white boats and all that is our mother. And I'm eighteen, with three spare tampons in my backpack, a cellophane of corn nuts and a river water bottle. How the election has set me free and I never ever have to do anything any adult tells me again because Trumpet has slain them all, the grown-ups are dead, we're all rogue now, like it or no. There was Ernie Landers and hope and belief, and I could have done it, I could have been what Daddy wanted, but that was then and this is now. Like the man said: *I used to care but that has changed.*

We left 1-15 just past Beaver, with its hokey I ❤ Beaver Truck Stop where you can get the bumper sticker with a fill up, onto Highway 20, into the snow banks and ridge line folds until you outright disappear, like driving off the face of the earth— that's what I did, you know, willingly drove off the face of the earth. Space got big. Sky mushroomed over the Bear Valley, red rock formations, Navajo sandstone glistening where snow melted into secret places and lay in seep holds for six million years before spilling out in a pool such as the first humans sipped from, water so sweet and good that you were drunk with it, the spider and deer and lizard, snake and wolf brother, your blood kith and kin come to the flow from deep dark quiet, water from another world.

From Kanab to Page, though the gut of the Colorado Plateau, to Glen Canyon, flooded forever by the blue Colorado, over the steel bridge with red rock canyon and far off stripe of silver water, there's no radio station and we don't have service. I've forgot CDs except two, Neil and Mom's, Iris Dement, with her sad hillbilly wail, I skip it, roll my window down, listen to the wind over my fingers.

Jack's dead in the passenger seat.

Not dead, conked out, his breath fogging the window. His parents will kill him, his mother with her mile long list of his faults. I remember her from Snake Paul's Episcopal Daycare when we were five and Daddy'd walk me up the flagstone sidewalk, past the little man with a bird on his shoulder and in through the huge oaken double doors and the food pantry always smelled like hot bread and cinnamon, up to the second floor nursery where Mary was, sweet Mary with her blue hair, she'd hug us close when our parents had left and the day would unwind just fine. We'd finger paint giraffes and there was chocolate milk time, and she'd read to us from a story that never ended about a bear who fell in love with a princess, and Jack would sing out *I am not a bear, I do not have black hair*. Jack, there he'd be. He could whistle. And we'd laugh like crazy, me and Jack, the part about the bear who didn't have black hair. Why can't I whistle?

Why did I never learn?

And one day, once upon a time, in a land far away where there were silver mountains washed over by golden sunshine, and the wings of mourning doves whistled far and wee, there was a wicked witch who'd stolen the young prince from the King's castle, and the girl he'd fallen in love with, who the Prince had give a golden ring wrapped in rose petals, she wept and cried and moaned until she turned into a bear with black hair and set out to find Prince Jacobi. And when she found him it was a Wednesday, a spaghetti day, their favorite because hot buttery bread was crusty on the plate, and there were meatballs and applesauce dusted with cinnamon, only the wicked witch came and took him from the feast, and he'd cried outside the nursery room door, and she'd hit him, the wicked witch, and it had hurt, you could tell by the sound. The girl-bear was furious, and the roar that rose inside her broke her into pieces, so she was just a little girl again, five years old in Snake Paul's Castle where in the sanctuary stained light fell on stone floors and I never knew why.

She'll kill him, Jack's mother.

After Snake Paul's, our lives conspired to intertwine twice, once by accident and the other by fate. I'm still not sure which was which—the accident or the fate. There was East High School, that day I was sitting by myself because the preps and Gabby Jensen had found out I wasn't Mormon and I got locked in the bathroom with *corrupt* written on the door in pink magic marker and I was thinking about lying about my age, joining the Air Force, getting the hell out of Dodge. He's sat with me, whistled the tune from *Bridge on the River Kwai*. Was that accident or fate? Jack finding me at the table that day when I was a Senior in high school, seeing my life through the wrong end of a telescope—or was it a rifle scope?

Daddy said for me to major in History. I majored in History. Daddy said apply to the Honors College. I applied to the Honors College. Answer the phone when he or Mom called. I answered the phone. Wash my sheets every Sunday. I washed my sheets. On Sundays, I stripped the extra-long dorm sheets and rode TRAX home to wash. Floss my teeth. Get up before ten. Don't skip class. Take my language placement exam before I forgot every blooming thing I'd ever learned in Spanish. Sign up for Alternative Spring Break. Write an essay for the Environmental Legacy Program. Pray. Vote. I could go on. I could. On and on and on and on. On the morning of the first snow, he called to tell me to run outside barefoot like we had for my whole life. *Good crazy*, he called it.

My roommates at Donna Eccles Fox Garff Residential Honors Living—DEFGRHL—were bitches. Supreme bitches. They all had bumper stickers with SUPREME in big red letters in case anyone forgot. The three of them had pledged Chi Omega and got in, and rubbed it in my face.

Halloween night, they held a social in our dorm suite, popped popcorn and heated apple cider, and when I walked into the living room that said *get out*, the space was for sisters only. They never dumped the trash. Month old pasta alfredo sat in a bowl beside a waffle beside something I wasn't sure about on the counter top. The sink was full of dishes on top of broken glass. Who knows about the dishwasher. The recycling bin runneth over. No one swept. The bathroom, don't even ask. So that's the state of affairs the day Mom paid a surprise visit, just out of the blue calls me from the lobby and says to ring her up, she wants to "see my space." She said that I didn't sound right, what was wrong with me? Were my roommates around? Could they meet?

And it was at that moment, Mom on her way up the elevator to doom and destruction she'd have to report back to Dad, who'd no doubt go apeshit so it would all hit the fan, when Jackson I'm-Not-A-Mormon Tripp rang my doorbell to ask me to Homecoming that very Saturday night.

In his right fist, a bouquet of yellow roses with a single red one shining.

Mom blushed when she saw him, figured out what was happening, and said "I was just bringing you this, like I promised." She gave me a basket of yellow pears from the backyard. "They bake really well."

"Same color as the roses. I'm Jackson," Jack said. "We went to Saint Paul's together. Remember me?"

Mom smiled. He was handsome. And she liked that. And I had about zero dates since who knows when. He saved me, Jack Tripp.

"You've grown up. Since Snake Paul's."

He reached to shake her hand, and she accepted. "You haven't aged a day," Jack said. "I forgot we called it that, Ms. Harvell. Snake Paul's." Jack could smile while he talked, how many people can do that?

"Renee," Mom'd said, and that was that. She left us to make our homecoming plans and never discovered the utter oblivion we'd wrecked on our fifth floor abode in Deaf Girl. That was fate, Mom meeting Jack while he offered me a bouquet of yellow roses. Or was it accident?

Like I said, I'm not sure there's a difference.

In Page, there's no food. Every restaurant has an hour wait, throngs of Chinese come to see the Grand in winter, snow on the rim. Finally we get a pizza with buffalo wings, this Navajo waitress with a big smile, and double ice-waters. Not so bad—for the starving. Our hotel room is big as a house, for some reason, the far window facing west, the canyon walls lit dimly all night long by the waxing Wolf Moon.

The sun's not fully over the rim when we drive out, a little stunned by the biscuits and gravy and scrambled eggs, fried potatoes, endless apple and orange juice at the

Best Western breakfast buffet. Our road heads south, paralleling the river. You can feel it out there, shining beneath the occasional flash of Moenkopi, Kayenta, we cut down through a shaded fall to Bitter Springs where, out of the blue—as these things come to me—we detour, hang a U-ey back toward Lee's Ferry, holy ground from that far off day ten years ago when I saw it all coming, though I didn't know it then—*how could I?*

There are two Navajo bridges at Lee's Ferry, one old and one new. Both are steel. Condors with numbers spray-painted on ten foot wings crouch up under them like gargoyles watching the hapless fools float by below them toward oblivion. The park rangers rely on these birds to seek out suicides because, as we learned in orientation before the Grand trip, everybody and their mother comes to the Grand Canyon to kill themselves because it's, well, the Grand fucking canyon. The carrion condors have telescope eyes, they feed on the corpses after making these huge swooping circles the rangers diagram on topo maps and send scouts to on horseback.

Tourists walk across the older bridge, though beware, the bathrooms are locked, and you'll have to go behind the bushes by the riverside, where a half-dozen others have left sticky toilet paper already that morning. There'll be a rattlesnake, a Grand Canyon pink, they call it. Mom walked with me until we saw the snake, that first time.

Tucked inside a stone wall by the locked up bathrooms, Daddy was riveted by the ten foot tall marble memorial to John D. Lee. He had that look on his face. We were about to head down to the put-in and wait for PRO to bring our rafts for rigging, just killing time, and we'd walked the bridge one end to the other. Then we tried the bathroom doors and the memorial was a jolt:

LEE'S FERRY

NORTHERN GATEWAY TO ARIZONA
FOR 54 YEARS—FROM 1873 TO 1927—
IS LOCATED SIX MILES UPSTREAM
FROM THIS BRIDGE.

THIS MONUMENT ERECTED
TO THE FOUNDER

JOHN   DOYLE   LEE

WHO WITH SUPERHUMAN EFFORT

AND IN THE FACE OF ALMOST
INSURMOUNTABLE OBSTACLES,
MAINTAINED THIS FERRY
WHICH MADE POSSIBLE THE
COLONIZATION OF ARIZONA.

FRONTIERSMAN, TRAIL BLAZER,
BUILDER, A MAN OF GREAT
FAITH, SOUND JUDGEMENT, AND
INDOMITABLE COURAGE.

AUTHORITY FOR ERECTION OF THIS MONUMENT GRANTED BY THE
STATE OF ARIZONA
1960

"One of these days I'm going to blow that up," Daddy said. "Mark my words." He spat, and at that second one of the spray-painted condors flapped pterodactyl wings over the blue river. It was number seven, a lucky number.

"Why?"

"Why not?"

He'd held out a hand, and I took it. I'd learn that Lee was the man who'd led the massacre of the Fancher party, who'd had them surrender to the white flag, then shot them all, even the littlest skulls with a bullet hole on the backside. There's a monument out there in a place called New Harmony, that keeps getting torn down and rebuilt. It's not my fight.

Jack and I walk out onto Navajo Bridge Number One. Halfway across, two black condors take form, one of which faces us, looks me straight in the eye from a rib of steel on the bridge my father will one day blow up, faces the rising sun, spreads wings to their full unbelievable span and stands shimmering before us, a moment that comes much later to represent this trip, the circle life makes.

The country has a lonely feel from there to Flagstaff, every few miles a mobile home built into the side of a dirt hill with smoke rising from the wood stove pipe on the roof, snow in place where shade lingers, no trees nor water anywhere to be seen. Where on earth do they get their firewood, these Navajo, their water?

Jack's done his homework, knows Highway 17's been closed and reopened south of Flag, two semi-trucks got wrapped up with each other in a foot of fresh snow. We drive off the archipelago and begin the three thousand foot fall off the plateau, the snow banks melting away to this stunning green cactus, the red gorge marking Sedona to our west, and then, an hour north of Phoenix, the saguaros I'd heard of but never seen. Like men, some of them, holding Pentecostal hands up, reaching green limbs toward the jubilate sky, a thing there was no words for, snow to saguaro.

It's Friday, I've missed Math. By Phoenix, the phones buzz like beavers. Jack's driving, he's a slow poke. I've traded Neil out for The Decemberists—Mom's fave. We saw them in concert at Red Butte, she gave Dad's ticket away at the front gate, he hadn't wanted to come even though the ticket cost sixty dollars, and you know how he is about money. Their number flashes, Mom and Dad's, I resist listening to the messages, and outside looks like we've driven off our earth onto another one where you can see forever and ever and the trees are all midget trees and there are no fences or clouds and I'm waiting for cactus, and then it comes.

I said, "Do you think they know we're gone?"

Taking the Outback was Jack's idea, both our parents drove them so we knew the gears and which side of the car the gas went in, and how much air should be in the tires.

He said, "Mom had Dr. Gattrell put a tracking device under this filling. She knows exactly where I am." He pointed to a back molar. A semi blew past. And then another.

"They only do that on dogs."

"Bow wow," said Jack. And he whistled. He could still whistle. "My tool box's in the trunk. I have pliers."

He gave me that look, Jack. We'd escaped, but to where?

I said, "My grandfather flew in yesterday. We're supposed to have early Thanksgiving. Him and Rose." The car smelled—we'd driven straight through. "I have to pee."

"Tell me who we're meeting. Me, too."

The next town was Casa Grande, sixty-seven miles from Tucson. "My dad's Uncle, Davey. He's a dwarf wrestler."

A sign announced ruins. Another, a rest area. "He wrestles dwarves?"

I said, "Turn here." It was a combination rest area and View Ruins From Sidewalk site, so we peed, then stretched our legs out on sidewalks that wound round kivas and lookout towers and a bench that faced south with a plaque in front of it that told the story of the Old Spanish Trail, how it was used for transport of goods to and from California, but mostly for slaves stolen from Indians.

"How much cash do you have?"

Jack said, "Thirty dollars."

"We could rob a bank."

"For sure let's do. Where's a bank?"

We had cards, they could track us by our cards. We hadn't thought of that, of course.

Bonnie and Clyde, we fly toward Mexico.

Highway 10 turned south and East toward a saddleback rock formation, an odd marker, it caught the eye from fifty miles away and I knew I was seeing a landmark that my grandmother Josephine had looked at and thought on from the other side in Tucson when she was my age, exactly, far from home and pregnant with Daddy. A girl still, really, I see her in my face.

Jack pokes a message to his berserk mom, the saguaros for real now, sixty feet tall and that saddle topped peak getting closer, my first semester of college behind me, that bitch Rashana and her stinky-ass bathroom, the two month old food rotten in the trash can for Daddy to find the one time he showed up to inspect, under the plastic bag. It fell out, fetid, when we dumped into the rubbish bin. I gagged. The smell took my breath. He'd just looked at me, that look. "You know you're better than this," he'd said. "Do you know that?"

Had she ever asked him that, Josephine?

It had come to stand for the whole mess behind me, the grades, Trumpet, the Dakota Pipeline at Standing Rock, the melting arctic and dying polar bears, the hottest year in history and the one before, bimbo blonde Gabby Jensen and the preps, the Mormon Church and how the lie in my head got bigger and bigger until I was the lie. I see her in my face, Grandma Josie, almost to Tucson, that smell behind me now for good and ever.

Orchards. The cactus gave way to these unexplainable fields on either side of Highway 10, that odd landmark peak on top of us now, what I'll learn are the Catalina Mountains growing to our south and east, 10,000 feet tall Mount Lemmon with a foot of fresh powder shining on it, what *she'd* seen when the labor pains came and who could know it was the onset of hemorrhage?

"*Picacho*," Jack said. "*Picacho*." He smiled, pounding the dashboard, alive for the first time in many miles. "It's goddamn *Picacho*."

Pistachio trees, a zillion of them, grew from the roadside away as far as you could see. The saddleback formation we've seen pulling us toward it since Phoenix, that's Picacho Peak, and there's a state park named for it, a road to the top. Jack said, "Let's do it," and Mom's Subaru made the climb in nothing flat. We could see Tucson from up there, where we were going and where we had been. I pictured these families arriving for the harvest, the music and aroma of roasting nuts, of fathers lifting sons to the stars by firelight, and it floors me that for all my life Daddy's been buying Mom pistachios for Christmas time, just as her own father had, and that some of them had dyed red shells against the green fruit, so that they're a Christmas tradition, pistachios, so that I know that these migrant families, they brought with them their manger scenes, baby Jesus in the rough hewn crib with the bright star towering above, Joseph and holy mother Mary, the braying donkey and calf. They brought makings for tamales to the camp where they picked pistachios that were dyed red for Christmas, Daddy's birthday. Surely grandmother Josephine came to know all this, so the peak upon which we gaze toward the city became a beacon of what would come, a hope, maybe? *Geronim*o, Jack said it, and we flew down onto Highway 10 through Red Rock and Marana and the Tortolita Mountains, Oracle Junction out there somewhere.

"He's old," I said. "The dwarf. We met at MaMa Josephine's funeral. In Arkansas. Where Daddy grew up." It felt like summer. My clothes were all wrong. I could smell myself.

Jack said, "We've crossed two states."

"Almost," I said.

Both our phones buzzed at once—his made a sound like a blender chop-chopping ice for a smoothie, a sound from my own story. "We could drive to Mexico," he said.

"Get married and rob banks. Fuck the grown ups."

Jack looked me through. It was another world out there. The light was different. He said, "*Right*."

I don't know why I said it, it seems like bad luck now. Arizona does not practice daylight savings, so back home it was five o'clock happy hour. Poppy and Rose and Mom were drinking vodka tonics in front of the news that was all about the godawful shock Trumpet's election had sent the markets into, how the trending catch phrase of the day was *twilight zone*, and all the protest marches going on from here to Timbuktu. All of that. Daddy was outside glowering, rolling cigarettes and smoking them one to a drink. They'd all be silly soon so, at least on my end, I was safe till tomorrow.

The cotton was a shock.

Outside Tucson, near a placed called Oro Valley, the fields were white as Utah snow banks with Arizona cotton. Cotton—the last time I saw it was in Arkansas when we were headed to MaMa's one last time, for that family photograph that sits on our fireplace mantel now, and we'd somehow got behind this funeral procession deep into Lonoke County where the stuff grew from way off all the way up to the front doors of these ramshackle houses and Daddy'd pulled over to the roadside, let the state trooper lead all these shiny American cars by. Mama'd cried. I don't know why. She'd been there before, Arkansas. Hell, they'd lived there, me too, but I don't remember. That farm house where I lost the pooh kite. The barn. The swimming pool where I'd swim in leaves from the hickories, and she'd come to us there in the Ozarks, MaMa. And we were on our way to see her one more time before she died, and got tangled in this funeral procession with a cotton field on both sides of the road. Daddy'd pulled over, the Reverend Jody Love playing blues out of Morrillton then. I got out, ran into it. Picked big fistfuls of the stuff and threw it in the air. Surely this would have been a comfort to MaMa Josephine, the cotton, grown by Tohono O'odham Indians outside Tucson when she was nineteen and pregnant with dad and it was 1960, the year of the big rains, when this Pineapple Express rolled through the great southwest and there were Old Testament floods and mayhem and she'd almost died in childbirth, the doctors walking out to the family and saying the mother won't make it, and the baby won't make it and nobody ever makes it in Tucson, with Picacho Peak off in the distance between Mexico and the way north. West, toward I don't know what.

Jack was a whole other deal. His mother tracked him by the dog chip in his tooth. We turned to a Mexican station outside of Tucson and the light going west was out of this world.

"This is where my Dad was born," I said. "This is sort of a homecoming."

"For you?"

I said, "In his place."

Jack let me drive the rest of the way in. We needed gas and directions to the bar where my Uncle Davey, the dwarf in Dad's black Bible, would meet us, and then? We had a reservation—that much I'd thought through, but the rest—who knew. It was up in the air.

"Welcome home, Lara's dad," Jack said.

Just then a giant sign rose up to announce the *Miracle Mile*.

The Saguaro National Park has an east side and a west. Our rental, the one I scored the night before last, is out this street called Broadway which runs straight by the University of Arizona with its gigantic football stadium, past this park where Native Americans—I guess Native Americans, Apache?—stood drinking, past used car lots and an Air Force base and sign that said South Tucson which is where we'd end up. The road went to gravel and we made the turns we were supposed to make, Freeman Road to Wentworth, and the gate with a Christmas wreath on it. There, behind a door that was unlocked, was where Jack and I'd stay for these few days, a corral down hill, with two dirty horses neighing at us, a heeler dog, carried our stuff through the front door, under which lived a six-foot rattlesnake, we'd learn. There was a six-pack left on the counter, a bottle of white wine. We opened windows and found the bed. Outside, a tree-high saguaro had an arrow shot through its crown. Mountains, the Catalinas, rose up in the distance, and south was Mexico—we'd driven to another country.

13. Josephine

Dear Lara,

Happy Birthday sweetie. There is so much I want to say to you, my whole heart is filled with love for you and hope that your life will be bright and happy and that someone will love you like there's no tomorrow. I'm old now. I feel older than I am. One of these days you'll understand this, though my hope is you never have to hurt like me, not ever. This lupus can go jump in the lake. It gets worse and then it gets better and then it gets worse. The medicine makes you loopy so you have to decide—loopy or hurt real bad. It's got a personality, the pain, you get to know it like a dog that's always pooping on your carpet, and you want to rub its nose in it, but it's an old dog, a family pet, that won't do any good. I've got Mom Dee—she tries, but prayer only goes so far, and our politics don't jive. She's never forgiven me working the campaign, and as far as she's concerned—and O.W., for that matter—Hillary's a witch, and she tells me I can spell it any way I want. You'll learn about politics one of these days, it's like this huge poker game that goes on for two years at a time, there's ginormous wins and losses and in-between hits and misses, so it gets in your blood and you live it and eat it and breathe it, and it's enough, maybe, to help you forget, for awhile, that your son, your flesh and blood, died so horribly in the car wreck, to keep you from picturing and thinking about it for awhile, seeing him there in his casket, I just can't go there.

So the campaign was, for me, a hoot, the headquarters downtown in Little Rock where all us Arkansas Travelers held our meetings and staffed the phone lines, and James Carville would kick a trash can from one end of the building to the other when something went bad. *It's the economy, stupid*, he wrote up on a poster board, so it became our motto, *it's the economy, stupid.* Bill'd walk in out of nowhere and give us hugs, and bring us tamales from Doe's across the street where all the FOBs had happy hour and planned strategies to beat Bush and his sidekick Quayle who spelled potato with an *e* in it.

Why am I telling you all this? I don't know. You've got to have something to live for, to love for. I'm talking to myself. You're so far away from me, granddaughter. I've got that picture framed, the one your mama took with her tripod, where we're all under that gazebo over to Day's Inn, and we're all waving at the camera—like there's somebody there! There you are sweet one, your hand in the air beside me, waving hello. The last time I ever saw your face.

When your daddy was born, I thought I'd never be alone again. My own daddy'd had to leave, Mom got a restraining order on him, there were others, and then Buddy Washer, your grandfather by blood, I ran away with him to Arizona, I don't know why. He was good-looking, had movie star teeth, and he told me his family was rich, that they owned this huge ranch outside Tombstone, and I guess they did one time, that's where Katy grew up, and I did meet her, she was flesh and blood and there was this story about her crawling up the chimney to hide from Geronimo, and I'm pretty sure it's true—imagine that, he'd skinned a white girl with a hunting knife, Geronimo. 1885 or something like that, which was 75 years before I met Katy, and she was eighty-something, so the timing works, it could be true. I heard the story from her own mouth the first time I met her. It was a long time ago, then, I was pregnant with your dad. Katy had his blue eyes and they twinkled. There was a dog, I remember, that kept hopping on and off the couch where Katy lay, a blanket over her, around Thanksgiving, I think. Buddy introduced me, then left us alone, that was her idea, that we be left alone.

And she looked at me through those milky blue eyes, a strand of still-auburn hair curling from her bun, and she took my right hand in hers, said, "I was wondering when you'd come."

It was a rock house, with a formation like a dragon's back behind it. A little river that curved under the cottonwood trees that were yellow that day, shining, the leaves falling like little helicopters. You'll know the place, it's in your blood. The brothers all played horseshoes out in the front yard—you could hear the dinging. The television was off, there was music from somewhere, maybe a car radio outside. 1960, I was twenty years old, pregnant, had run away from my family to this strange desert with its saguaro and Gila monster and blue sky. Mount Lemmon always shone in the distance, snow-capped, so odd in the heat even in November. Actually I was nineteen, about to turn twenty, my birthday's at Thanksgiving. Nineteen, how old Jimmy was. How old you'll be one day. And I'd just arrived, just like you, and Katy held my right hand in hers. I wanted to believe in her, that she was kind-hearted, the first sane one of them yet, the Washers.

"You knew I was coming?"

She nodded, Katy, had this way of smiling that made you feel it.

"Why of course I did, honey. Ever since I was a girl, five or six, and Father made me climb into the chimney. He hid us kids there. Only I crawled out and no one saw."

The light was different, it had a shine to it, a thereness, and it washed in the front windows that were wavy, that old timey glass, like yours, Lara, your front room. Little motes flowered between us, swirled when we breathed. In a month your daddy'd be born, and I'd run from Buddy soon after, but at that moment, on that day while Katy held my hand, it was all still wide open in front of me. There was hope, still. I was nineteen and in love. It could go either way.

"They were barefoot, the Indians. Laying in the shade of the big cottonwood. Hungry.

They were beat. They looked at me. And one said something. He moved his hand to his mouth, said the word again. And I knew. I walked back to the house and no one saw. I was invisible now, and I knew you were coming, that you'd be able to see me, that you'd understand why I did it."

Outside, someone threw a ringer. A door shut, opened, and shut again. I was thirsty. I lived on ice water then, when I was pregnant and it really was the desert, the air so dry that your whole body up and cracked, your toenails and hair and nose, everything sort of withered there.

"There was a cellar where we kept napalitos and the fruit from prickly pear, cantaloupe and chili peppers, tomatillo and eggs. It was cool and there was no light. I remember because I had to wait for my dark vision. I had to wait to be able to see. You could smell it from the doorway, the cantaloupe. I carried it to the tree, gave it to the man who'd said the strange word and moved his hand to his mouth."

She held my hand, rested it in one of hers, and brought the other on top, the way some people have when they want to soothe, show they care. "You were watching me then, and the one who'll come after you, all of us Katys, we were there, offering him fruit from our cellar.

They were hungry, the last wild Indians in the world. They'd run a hundred miles to get here."

I asked her how. "How was I there?"

"He drew a knife from a scabbard. Up at the house, I heard Daddy yell. He cut it, the melon, scooped the seedy mush from the center out with one hand, slurped from the hole, smiled. '*Ashagoteh*," he said, and then, 'thank you.'"

Katy shut her eyes, and I felt her tremble.

"He passed the food to his people, made a circle in the dirt, a handprint, and he blessed me. Geronimo. I would live long, he said. Here was where my great-great grandson's medicine would be, on this spot, this circle. The last Katy would come here, come barefoot along the river, and the medicine would be hers. Time would start again."

The moment passed. I should have asked her what it meant, the Geronimo story. How I was there. Who came after me. I'm not sure. Maybe it's about mercy or forgiveness or kindness.

Turning the other cheek. Feeding the hungry. Charity. I've puzzled over it all these years and the answer's not come—or maybe it has. After Jimmy died, a part of me went with him, but not all of me. There was Trace, her part of me lived, and there was Joey who, when I first held him to my face, it was like lifting myself to myself. If that makes any sense at all. And maybe that's what Katy's story was all about, this minute when you'll be lifted out of yourself to yourself.

That's what I'm believing. Yeah, I believe.

Joey had it carved on back of my tombstone, go see.

I believe.

See—I told you, either hurt or loopy.

14. Josephine

January 16, 2002

Dear Lara,

When the monsoons come, the desert transforms to a sea of delirium. Delirious. Fire Chalice. Scarlet gilia. Paintbrush. Penstemon—purple and blue. Violet. Bluebell. Flax and Aster. Monkey flower. Phlox. False Solomon's Seal. Death camas. The cactus flowers white as magnolias the springtime when Joey learned to crawl and we'd drive some days out into the desert, just the two of us and breathe it in, and once a flock of storks flew over with the sun on their wings, so they all converged into this wonderful being that hung on the horizon for a long, long time. What I'm saying, granddaughter, is that there is great beauty where you least expect it, but I'm sure you already know this, or that you will when you're old enough to *need* to know. I had to learn for myself, and it's been slow-going. When I was eighteen, just before I met Buddy, me and this girl named Colleen, we stole a car and went night driving on gravel roads outside Danville, out near the hunt club where Daddy cut his leg off—we just turned the radio on and drove, smoked cigarettes, stuck our arms out the windows and our whole heads so breeze whipped our hair ever' which way—I'll never forget that free feeling like nobody on earth would ever own me, and I'd always be able to decide which way was up and which was down. I'd be my own boss.

Colleen turned a curve and my door came open. I fell out. I could see the taillights red and twinkling, brighter when the brakes were on. It wasn't bad enough for skin grafts, but close. I remember laying on the gurney, the sound a piece of gravel makes when it's dropped onto the metal, thirty-three in all. Doc said I'd set a record for the most rocks to come out of anyone's butt for the whole history of St. Mary's in Russellville. There'd been this wild exuberance of being young and free and deciding for myself, and then I fell out the car door and butt-slid twenty feet on a gravel road. That's how love is—freedom and then falling.

It hurt like hell.

Buddy'd married a Mexican woman and had children with her. He kept that family across the border. Turns out his daddy did the same thing. All Washers had second families across the border. What was my problem? Get with the program. And the work thing? Sometimes he actually did go to work—it wasn't always all day drinking beer at that wrestler's bar. And the lies? The story about his little daughter whose mother'd been killed in a car wreck. How she missed her mommy so much that she couldn't speak and I could love her, wouldn't I love her so she'd be better and talk again? I ran away from Arkansas to be the mother of an orphaned mute who Buddy'd conjured from thin air. It was a good story. Couldn't I just appreciate that? A good story? They ate dog. What's so bad about that? Dog, goat, what's the difference? And if I didn't like it, what was I going to do about it? Say? If I so much as thought about leaving Buddy Washer, he'd take Joey someplace where I could never find him, so how about them apples? For that matter, there were places he knew in the desert that weren't on any map. He could take me there and show me, and who would ever find me? Who?

Every time the bus stopped, El Paso, Abilene, Ft. Worth, Dallas, Texarkana, Hot Springs, Little Rock, Joey wrapped in a blue blanket, nursing still, I'd remember how it felt when he said he'd take him from me, Joey. That if I did get away he'd track me down, find me anywhere, I could run but I could not hide. He was coming, not far behind, I knew that, in my heart, I knew.

O.W. Harvell was 6' 2" and 240 with a Burr flat top. He drove a bread truck, and I was hungry, was I ever hungry, the day we met, hungry to get on with my life, to not see Buddy behind every window shade, outside every open window, in my dreams and waking, he was always there, about to take Joe from me to a place on no map. I'd started painting again, nothing much, water colors, pastel, some charcoal. Buddy came dressed as the postman one day. He said he had a letter from a judge awarding him custody. Liar. Mama came home and called the police. They arrested him, shoved him in a car and drove away. There was a tornado that day—the last day I ever saw Buddy Washer.

And that's how I went west and why I didn't stay. How I got back home and hooked up with O.W., who adopted Joey, gave him his name. I don't know how much your dad's told you about all that, how we married and divorced three times, about the fights, the godawful knock-down drag outs that Joey and Jimmy listened to through walls—it's a wild ride, this life. Trace was born, we made it through. I don't dwell. I don't know why I'm spilling my guts to you this way Lara. Your four years old now, beautiful and sweet and bright-eyed honey. I can't tell you what it meant to have you and your mom and dad home that year, in that big nice house where we had Thanksgiving dinner and that roaring fireplace and a guest bedroom, the barn and pastures and wild turkeys waltzing across the front yard. That meant the world to me, that Joey came home like that, a professor and all, with his own office at ArkaTech. One of these days you'll know, the child becomes your life, all there is, finally, between you and the world. When he got the job, he called up and said, "Mama, I'm coming home."

It was enough.

It would have been enough.

Then the business with his injury happened, and all that stuff about the mass murderer and the Love family—your mom never did like it. "People are named Peck Titsworth," she said to me one time. "What in god's name is a Peck Titsworth?"

So y'all moved back to Utah, and Buddy got his wish, both my sons gone now.

But in your heart you always carry part of a person you love, so you're all here with me, this second, while I'm writing to you right now. I've been down, but I'm getting better. It's January here in Lonoke. It snowed yesterday, and I started laughing. A cardinal flew into the pear tree, so bright it hurt my eyes, and I remembered how we used to make snow cream with sugar and vanilla, how my daddy'd wake me up on a snow morning just like MaMa Stepwell had woke him up when he was a boy. And we'd run outside in our PJs, barefoot, whoop and holler, it's what we always did for the first snow. Mom thought we were crazy, bumpkins, and she'd tell Daddy so to his face, that look that was part smile and part not, and he'd say damn right we're crazy, *good crazy*, and warm our feet by the space heater, make chili later in the day, grate cheddar on top, cornbread on the side. So this cardinal flew into the tree out back, and it hurt my eyes, and it all came whizzing back, my childhood, my life, everything that's ever been funny or joyful or magic, and I stood up, sister, just inside the bay window, took the slippers off my lupus-swollen feet, stepped out to meet it, the rest of my life.

Why I'm reaching to you now, Lara, is I feel something coming, and I'm afraid.

I don't know how to explain it except to say that there's a darkness I feel coming. O.W., your grandfather, and I, we're not good right now. I've made mistakes along the way, during the campaign, I met somebody. Live while you're alive, that's what I say. I've lived and I've loved.

I've paid. My time's coming just like everyone else. I'm sixty-one years old. I've lived a life. That night Clinton won, at the old State House there in Little Rock, a handful of us gathered out on the veranda with the new president, the hoopla dying down some. Somebody'd brought a Cuban cigar, a Cohiba, that Bill lit and we passed it around out there in the dark, the fireworks going off over the river. I imagine my love like a steamboat on that muddy river, blowing west through Oklahoma, through Kansas into Colorado where the headwaters are a sky high mile above me now, this second, writing to you, sending my love, hoping with my whole heart that you'll be kept safe, that you'll be happy, granddaughter, that you'll know love in your life and not get broken because of it, that you'll remember me and know how much I love you.

Katy *knew.*

Love with all of my heart,

MaMa

p.s., Lock your car door when you go on a joyride, live with your whole heart, like it's the last day everyday. I've left you a sign. Don't be scared.

Go love, honey. mmj

15. Davey

Just before she spoke, as the words formed on her lips and the old circle verged
on closing as my brother had ever dreamed it would one day, I remembered
the sun-drenched November afternoon when I drove the girl's grandmother
Josephine to Mission San Xavier del Bac to pray for the birth of her unborn
son. It had been her birthday, Josephine's. Buddy'd disappeared again who
knows where. She wore pearl earrings he'd wrapped before leaving, a note
swearing their authenticity. Huge, she was into her third trimester and sort of
waddled through the beat front doors where the full frontal assault of all that
Catholic friar mysticism came at us all at once—too much for me, really, even
now, the thought.

"It's beautiful," she said. "This is where I'm supposed to be. I know it."

She'd said it under the bas relief painting where someone's playing a lyre and
on the other side of the sanctuary, a pale hand holds a feather, writing on air, a tablet,
history of something, and there were candles burning on either side and down front,
and I got that creepy feeling from all those prayers.

"Davey," she said. "Can we buy three of those?"

"Candles?"

"It means something to me."

I was working then, a little. The odd ring match on Saturday night, reffing some.
What I'm saying is I had some pocket money, not a lot. In the visitor's center, candles
cost a buck apiece.

I bought three, one with this priest on it—I don't know what he was doing. "How
do you light it?" I asked the clerk, who was pretty.

"With fire," she said, smiled.

"How's 'at?"

"You figure," she said, smiled again. There were wood sticks inside, light those off already lit candles, that's what she said, added, "There's a stool at the foot of the wooden man."

A stool at the foot of the wooden man?

It was one of those lines that comes back on you, years later, when one of the bearded Ringo brothers is tearing your head off and you wonder why in hell, why in the devil's hell you ever took up wrestling or was born a dwarf on the borderlands between countries, the hell with all of it, and then the line came, *there's a stool at the foot of the wooden man*, and it dawned on you that if you could figure out that one thing, the heart of mystery beating in that line, then you'd be healed for once and all, and the truth of your soul would be visible, and people'd see you as if you'd grown to a normal height and they'd look you in the eye, and all would be forgiven.

Inside, the sanctuary had grown dark and strange, and the candlelight glowed in the eyes of the painted saints, it sparked in the marble footings and carven alter, the whole of the inside of the place laid out for the stations of the cross and high above the sainted priest himself, Xavier, who the Indians worshiped as *tunkasila*, mediator between heaven and earth.

In a front pew on the right-hand side, Josephine had fallen to her knees. She was praying in real live words that I remember to this day in her voice, the sweet vowels rolling, and she didn't ask many things for herself, but for the boy who flew our way for a Christmas birth, that his coming would be safe and she could take care of him in a good way, that her milk would come, and that her mother would make it here safely and that they could for god's sake get along. That her daddy and his big-butted wife would have a safe travel here from Arkansas, and that they could somehow find a way to get along with the Washers—who must be the strangest people on earth. She was crying, the girl. Sobbing between pieces of prayer. I knelt beside her. She said, "Thank you, Davey. You'll always be special to me for this."

Behind us, on the pew, candles clinked together. She talked to God like she knew him, and was there was this beseeching in her voice, this utter want and need and hard sadness. Any God that was worth his salt would surely hear her and give what she asked.

"Be with me," she said. "Be with this child."

There was an Indian manger lit up on a wooden table in the eastern nave, many candles guttering, so Indian Joseph and White Buffalo Calf Mary knelt before the holy Indian Jesus in his juniper manger, surrounded by burros and wise men Indians and a saguaro cactus which had grown in the shape of the cross. The baby Indian Jesus lay on an *O'odham* buckboard cradle beside a canupa and sweet grass, peyote buds and the ceremonial wine the ancestors had concocted to send them into spinning fits, where they communed with the other side and brought it back dripping from their lips. A symbol materialized in the airy light above the Indian nativity. I knew I'd never forget it, a black maze shaped into the form of a circle with a path that led distinctly to a center that was dark as the space inside a light socket, and above this, in the holy entrance to the kiva, a man the same color as the center space, presiding over, mediating between. Picture language, a way to read for those who couldn't read, who needed a holy man to breathe the martyrs and holy men to life.

"God, will you be with my husband," the girl said. And here the sob came from a place so deep inside her that I thought I'd break down right there, turn loose of my tongue and join her voice and call out to a God who'd dwarfed the universe. "Bring him home to me and this child. Lord, God. In the name of Jesus."

And it was here, just as those words escaped her lips that I heard another voice floating through the candlelight, a singing beyond music that was true and beyond reproach. I didn't know the words. They were bigger than me. *Domini. Jehovah.* The word made flesh.

It was her birthday, Josephine. A Tuesday, 29 November, 1960. We'd driven out to the rez where the Mission San Xavier del Bac shone white under the blue sky, the plaster on its Gothic domes, we'd learn, made from lime and cactus juice, a bell ringing clear and loud over the wide desert, the cemetery up the way, medicine wheels pierced by the cross where hung the Indian Jesus bleeding from his cactus thorn crown, the scarlet gilia flowering, the spear wound in his side opening to the darkness that is man.

Into the east nave, to the Tohono nativity, we carried the candles encased in glass. Many burned on a rack. Josephine placed two beneath the Indian messiah, then one in between. She lit a wooden stick from the manger. Three candles danced to life. She leaned down and hugged me, so I could smell her shampoo and her skin and wondered how Buddy could be such an absolute fuck up.

I said, "There's a stool at the foot of the wooden man." All I could think of, it was all I had to give.

She tilted her face, looked at me with those brown earth eyes, her mascara running. "This way," she said.

Until now I had not even noticed that we weren't alone. A line snaked from the front alter beneath the bearded saint on high, into the west nave, where in a wooden resting place lay a figure under a blanket woven of threads that caught light and held it. A brown woman knelt before the wooden effigy. She kissed its hands, its feet, then, as every other pilgrim to this shrine, placed both hands under the skull, lifted.

Only one with a pure heart, I'd learn, could lift the head of the wooden man.

One by one we made our way, kissed the feet, placed hands beneath the head. Before me, Josephine, my brother's wife, a girl with child. She stood there on the stool weeping hot tears, the saint's head bobbing in her hands.

When my time came, I climbed up on the stool, kissed the feet, the hands, placed palms under the slick-worn head, an uncanny voice singing *Domini, Jehovah*, words that whistled through my skin.

Outside was a hill with a cross on top, and a secret grotto where the blessed Virgin had once appeared. We didn't know that—the blessed Virgin appearing part. It was just a hill with a cross on top. People were climbing the path that circled it, working their ways up the *camino* to the cross. Navaho and Tohono O'odham families, maybe some Apache and Pima, they were cooking frybread for sale in the parking lot in front of the mission. In the crisp air, the fire-charred bread smelled good. There was the aroma of melted cheese and grilled meat.

"The baby's kicking. Feel," the girl said.

She held my hand to the turquoise blouse, the mission so bright behind us that I had to shade my eyes, and I felt nothing—maybe one has to feel a baby kick from the inside out?

"Maybe it's hungry." The frybread smelled like heaven. Off to the south, Black Mountain, Mexico, Nogales where Buddy kept Socorro and his other family in a yellow stucco with chickens scratching in the front yard.

"He wants us to climb up there. We're supposed to see something. Right up there."

"How about I buy frybread. They'll stuff it if you like."

Her twentieth birthday, she'd planted flowers in front of their cottage, I don't know what kind. They never came up. She was no gardener. But she knew who she was and what she needed, Josephine Stepwell Washer.

We walked the path that circled the holy hilltop. There were shrines, little places where someone had tucked a photograph and plastic flowers under a rock where lizards lay in the cool shade, tasting the air for monsoon rains. North and a little east, Tucson was plain as day, the tallest buildings gleaming with the Catalina Mountains rising behind, Mount Lemmon and Summerhaven with a touch of snow already—ten thousand feet up there, two miles. November 29th, the girl was a touch over eight months and Buddy was eldest of us Washers, this would be the first grandchild. My mother, Vi, this child was to somehow make right the wrongs she'd suffered at Daddy's hands, her work in the prison, her crazy offspring of which I was one, this child had been promised in a dream, and I was to take care of the girl at all cost. And most of all I was not to let her run like some of the others had. This one stays, Vi demanded, don't let her run.

"Tell me about your brother. What makes him tick?"

We'd circled the hill with the cross on top one time entirely, and had just started the second round, the smell of frybread wafting up at us from the parking lot. It was some question: my brother.

"He needs something to believe in."

The girl nodded in that way she had, like she understood everything you said in some deep inside way. What were we looking for? What were we supposed to see?

"What else?" She had a bright smile. No really, she could be the happiest person in the room.

"Love. He needs to be loved."

Josephine stopped walking on the side of the hilltop facing Tucson. To our right was a grotto, invisible from the ground, and barred. We were alone. There was no one but me and Jo and the baby kicking inside. A bronze plaque said *Here Appeared the Blessed Virgin who Intercedes For Us With Christ The King.*

Photographs of everyone you can imagine were taped up around the plaque, on the bars and ground inside the grotto. There was money and offerings of all sorts, pints of tequila, candles.

Prayers for the infirm, the drunk, the lost.

Maybe they *were* real, the pearl earrings Buddy'd wrapped for her to open this morning, twentieth birthday gift from a husband gone AWOL. They glittered in each ear, set in silver, lit her face.

She was lovely.

She slid the delicate hoops from each ear, held them gleaming to the sun, said *Hail Mary, full of grace. Never was it known that anyone who fled to thy protection, implored thy help, sought thy intercession, was left unaided. I fly to thee, mother, sinful and sorrowful. Mother of the world incarnate, hear me. Protect my son. Please speak to Him for us.*

She lay her birthday earrings on a white stone at the foot of the plaque announcing the appearance of the Blessed Virgin. "Please," she said. "Please."

"We all need to be loved," she said, and left them lay.

Fifty-six years ago this month. We walked together then, circling the cross-topped hill. The world seemed big around us, that's how it felt. Not in a way to make you feel small, but part and parcel of. A true panorama in all directions: north toward Picacho Peak with its odd saddleback pointing the way to Phoenix; south toward Buddy and old Mexico where Geronimo had hidden his people; east toward Arkansas where the girl'd run after it all blew up, and we'd follow her, Buddy and I; and west, the end of the line, where the roads run into the sea. She reached a hand to me. There was kindness in her eyes. I wished she was my sister.

In the parking lot I ordered frybread from a family with many children playing with Tonka toys in the dirt, speaking their language, laughing and squealing, one of them eyeing us while the bread cooked, its sweet smell a thing I'd never forget, and I don't think she ever forgot either.

How I drove her to Mission San Xavier del Bac on her birthday, the candles and the frybread. The stool at the foot of the wooden man.

On Christmas Day she hemorrhaged and the surgeon kept walking out and saying that one or both of them wouldn't make it. There were carolers. Her daddy drank whiskey. He gave me some. And I thought about those candles burning in the church. The tenor of her prayer. The earrings at the foot of the plaque. *Dear Mary, please speak to Him for us.*

All this flies through my head when the girl materializes in the door, about to speak the words and close the old, old circle, her face so like her grandmother's that my heart misses a beat. I could die this second.

And never know.

15. Lara

Jack's phone's going off like a drunken Indian. I don't know why I said that, it's not like me.

But his mom's apeshit. She's filled the box with messages telling him to get his variously described arse home this second, right now, to find the Greyhound Bus Station where she's wired him a ticket and have not one more thing to do with that hussy Harvell girl. We're not right for each other. She's called the police. There's a missing persons report out—we're wanted.

There'll be heaven to pay. Worse. He's a good kid, Jack. We're eighteen, together. From a million miles away, I'll remember how he grinned sideways when the phone lurched into "Sweet Home Alabama," the billboard announcing MIRACLE MILE, how we took the off-ramp to end our road trip not five miles from where this story all began—me and Jack, wild and eighteen the year grown-ups forfeited the world, and everything was fair game. From here on out, Katy bar the door.

Tucson, for me, has always stood for where Daddy was born, this mythical place where what he called his blood father's people lived, where this ranch existed somewhere with a cottonwood tree where Geronimo'd eaten cantaloupe while kids hid in a fireplace chimney. There was cactus, and you could see a mountain with snow on it, and there was good Mexican food. Indians lived close by—there was a reservation or something. It was a long way from Arkansas. There were Catholics. Missions. The Spanish Trail. Friars. Peyote. Wrestling was big. Dwarves wrestled in masks and had their own bar named after one of their own. Charro's was where Buddy Washer had shot snooker when he was supposed to be at work as an electrician, and grandmother Josie had found out and took Daddy away. Buddy'd followed. There'd been trouble. He attempted kidnap while impersonating a postman. Mom Dee'd had him thrown in jail. He had to pick peas. He'd promised to come to Daddy's high school graduation, and didn't. Daddy'd talked to him on the phone. He had a funny accent. When they moved west, he'd mailed a ceramic Indian stuffed full of weed. Long black hairs were mixed with skunk weed in a quart size baggie wrapped in fabric softener cloths. The hairs belonged to his sister, Daddy's Mexican sister, the one from his father's other family. She was Buddy's right hand man, this Mexican sister. When MaMa drowned, the dwarf uncle showed up at the funeral. He was my uncle. I saw Daddy in his face. He called me cutie. Daddy'd called Buddy to tell him about MaMa, only his father'd screamed at him on the phone, wished him dead, I think. Daddy was supposed to have come down and met the family, but he hadn't. He hadn't showed. Chickens come home to roost, he said. Just a while back, Daddy found the obit—the name of the church and the cemetery. He was Catholic—my grandfather. An Air Force man with good teeth and wavy hair, a tendency toward alternative facts.

The dwarf lived.

We were meeting him today, this very afternoon, in fact, at Charro's, which was not in Tucson, but South Tucson, which is a whole other story, let me tell you. Because I'd been an idiot and rented a guest house at a ranch in Saguaro National Park because it sounded cool and I'd always pictured cactus when I thought of the place. And the Catalina Mountains were just to the north, the website said, you could see snow this time of year. There were horse trails through the park and Native American guides. That sort of thing. But South Tucson was another world—and one that we ultimately had great difficulty finding, even using Jack's phone to navigate, the thing going off every other second for him to get his fourteen-adjectived ass home.

"Broadway runs into 6th Ave. Old Nogales Road," Jack says. "Make a left."

Mom's car smells like road trip, and there was no good music. The check engine light blinked and then went off and then blinked on. I make the left on 6th and pretty soon the signs are all in Spanish, winos and pawn shops and barred gas stations. "We're getting close. Look for a plasma center."

"It's all numbers," Jack says.

"What's all numbers?"

He squints at the map, holds the iPhone this way and that. "6th to 32nd to something. Charro's has a sign. Turn left." I turn left.

"Turn left again." I turn left again.

Jack says, "There."

In front of us, a white sign with black letters—CHARRO'S. A stray dog lifts its leg on the skeleton of a bike chained to a grocery cart, the yellow pee in squirts.

Across the street, sure enough, a plasma center, next to an all-night drive-through liquor. A trailer park named Vista Court with a view of Mount Lemmon. Ground Zero, where it all began.

When I look back on that time in my life, through the wide end of the telescope seeing back through the skinny, from wherever this is all taking me, will I think to recall my world and how it was happening from the outside in? Will I think to recall the election, how Ernie Landers—a Jewish, atheist, hippy—had lit us all up, so five, ten thousand showed up at This Is The Place State Park and listened to him talk for three hours sticking it to the man, tearing down Wall Street where the Occupy Movement took its first breath? He breathed fire and brimstone on the ten men who owned half the wealth of our country, talked about ending the perpetual wars for oil, about how climate change was a cliff we were bats out of hell driving toward, how we ought to rebuild our roads and schools, and there should be free college for anyone willing to work. He hollered, lost his voice, got it back and more. The Dakota Access Pipeline Water Protectors had kicked it up a notch by then and Jane Fonda'd jumped into the fray. Neil Young—he wrote a dozen songs for the movement and started this band called Promise of the Real with Willy Nelson's sons—and five thousand vets of war traveled to the Cannonball River in God's own blizzard, strapped on body armor and double-dog dared the police or the hired mercenaries to try that dog siccing shit again, the midnight water cannons when it was twenty degrees, the shrapnel bombs, the noise torture. The Lakota Nation, Nakota, Dakota—hell, the whole of Indian nations—stood with Standing Rock, and they shut the pipeline down, if only for a while. How I'd been a Nasty Woman for Halloween, with a plastic machete with Trumpet's Lumpet written on it in fake blood. I was eighteen and big shit was going down. Professor Newell had us memorize "The Second Coming" by William Butler Yeats, and we all said it together, and it all just steam rolled over us and kept on rolling—*what rough beast, his hour come round at last, slouches toward Bethlehem to be born.* Trumpet was a knife in the back. He won. I mean people voted for this guy. Build a wall. Ban the Muslims. Hate your neighbor. Cheat a friend. Grab them you know where. The don't-give-a-damners ruled the world. Why not steal a car, get the hell out of Dodge? Go hang with dwarves and dog eaters, cast my lot with these? Trumpet won and the shit went down, and things didn't really matter for a while. That's how it was for a whole lot of us then.

Jack's scared. He wasn't Mormon, but he's never been in a bar—there's like five in Salt Lake, and you have to have a membership, and they build these walls called Zion curtains at burger and fry joints like Squatters and Purple Henry and Redrock Brewing, so no one could see a drink being poured, as if that was somehow worse than a carload of kids driving to Wendover, getting married so they could screw without sin, getting divorced before they drove home the same night, but no eye shall see the abomination of alcohol. We weren't bar people, me and Jack, and we stand outside the door for a while before going in. I'm certain those noisy men on the other side of the glass door saw us, me and Jackson Tripp with his phone battery finally fried, thank be, outside Charro's in South, Tucson, Veteran's Day, a week after what was maybe the last election there'd ever be for President of the United States of America.

Everyone was quiet. Behind me, Jack's breath caught in his throat.

The dwarf who was my Uncle Davey is on a stool halfway down this wooden sawdusted bar with photographs of men wearing boas and feathered headdresses, pythons and scarlet head masks, and even one, I saw straight away, of the orange peckerhead commander and chief whose name will not be spoken.

The silence gets real loud, but still we stand there, frozen on our feet, a gravitational ripple, and I know that whatever happens next, nothing will ever be the same for me—or anyone who knows me—again.

Through the vacuum time makes, we walk to him, and it seems like forever, all those faces turned on us, the eyes like some great wanting.

"Uncle Davey," I say. "I'm Lara."

And at that moment the pinball machines ding and the jukebox plays "I'm Walking the Floor Over You," and the snooker balls clack together on green felt. All the urinals in back flush at the once, and there's that spewing sound the tap makes when its primed on its keg. He stands down off the stool and smiles, nodding his head the way Dad does when he wants you to know he's paying attention. "You've grown up, girl," he says. "What can I get you?"

"Mr. Washer," I say, and hold my hand out to him. "This is my friend Jack. Jack Tripp."

A TV wired up in the corner played an Arizona Wild Cat basketball game—they were playing the Utes, clobbering them, already, in the second quarter.

His hand is warm, big as mine. His breath smells like beer. He wears no beard. Didn't dwarves wear beards? He's handsome, actually, familiar and strange and something else.

"Davey," he says. "You can call me Dave. Dirty D, if you like."

"Mr. Dirty D," Jack says, shakes his hand.

"We're not twenty-one, Uncle Davey."

We take a stool on either side of him, Uncle Dave, Jack on the right and me on the left, this huge long cracked mirror in front of us, with about a thousand wrestlers framed and hanging above, all signed—Mad Russian, Hay Hauler, the Cochise Twins, there's a ton of them. "It's free beer for Veterans Day. You a veteran, Tripp?"

Davey wears a big ring on one finger of his right hand, gold with a red stone. Hank Williams turns into a woman with a hillbilly voice who's singing about socking it to the Harper Valley PTA.

"A couple Co-colas, Chopper. Ever' one's a hero today, right?"

The bartender wipes the space in front of me with a white towel, flaps a cardboard coaster with a big, black C on it in front of me. "Can do, Dirt. You want a Slim Jim, Missy?"

"Lara says you've been in the movies," Jack says, white-faced, a foot taller than Uncle on his stool.

Davey's got a cigarette burning in the ashtray in front of him, a tall glass with a handle beside a piece of paper with a short list on it. Chopper sets our Cokes on coasters, refills Davey.

"Pickled egg?" he says. "Pork rind? Where'd you park?" Chopper says.

"Down the street."

"What you driving, sweets?"

"A Subaru."

"What year?"

"2005."

"Is it your car?"

"Yes," I said.

"You got papers on it."

"Why do you ask, *garçon?*" Davey says. "This is my niece. Buddy's granddaughter. She's just driven here from Timbuktu with this Mr. Tripp."

Chopper nods at the door. "Black Magic's rifling her glove box out there this second. Just saying."

He excuses himself, Uncle D., and Jack says what do we do now. His mother's gone ballistic and wired him a Greyhound bus ticket and he's to be on the northbound tomorrow or else. She wants to know what's got into him. Have he and that girl got into trouble? Has he done something he'll regret?

I tell Jack that I need him here, that I can't do this right now without him, that the world's gone crazy. "I have family here I've never met, Jack."

Jack says, "Why?"

It's not a question I'm ready for. I don't know what it means—to have family and not know. It's spin the bottle weird. I'm an only child, and that means I play the part of anyone that could have been and wasn't, or was but is no more. An only child in Mormon City—throw a rock and you'll hit somebody with eight brothers and ten sisters. Think about it, unclean and insufficient. Who are my people? That's what I want to know. Who?

"This is crazy. Crazy-crazy."

He says, "Remember that time we crashed in the snow. At Alta. After the gold rush blizzard?"

Chopper, who wears a name tag that says Ellen, sets a pickled egg in front of me on a napkin and another in front of Jack. He sets a salt shaker in between us beside Davey's full beer.

I say, "Yeah."

"The pixie dust was floating in the air. And we were on top of snow mountain. You were buried, toast. And I said good crazy?"

He's looking at me, Jack. There we are. A bar that I won't know is a dive, until the next time I come back, or the next, Tucson, Arizona, where Daddy was born. There was family out that door, people I'd never met who shared my blood. Later, I'll learn that MaMa Josephine wasn't the only one, she wasn't even first. The Washers, Buddy even, had hauled girls here from all over, borne across the desert on a raft of lies, only to land in front of a busted out trailer door beside the plasma center, the car overheated, a dwarf come stumping up with a water hose spurting in his hands. Children had been born, Daddy wasn't the only one. I'll learn of a whole tribe of wayward Washer kids, the people who eye you at rest stops, who ask you for fifty cents outside the liquor store, that glint in their eyes. I never told Daddy, about the lost tribe wandering in the desert.

"You said it was a sign." Jack breaks a hunk of the stinking egg, salts the yellow yolk, eats it. "What happens now?"

The place has a feel, like its this space ship sailing along in its own galaxy, the beat and ragged hustling each other through space and time, dodging black holes and quasars, free cold beer for vets. A few stared, looked away. Jack whose not a Mormon, he nods, wearing that look he has, goofy goofy us, why *were* we here?

"*Look*," Jack says.

In front of us, wearing this huge championship belt and buckle, a young Dirty Davey Washer, aka Little Lord Fontelbury. He smiles, the eyes dead ringers for Daddy's. It's him, my flesh and blood, for reals.

Uncle Davey has us drive him to this place called Guadalajara where they have good margaritas and homemade salsa made at your table while you pick ingredients. The place—it was loud and colorful, lots of blues and greens and *amarillo* with the smell of corn *tortillas y queso y flautas y magaritas con sal y virgin para* you and *mi amigo Jackson Tripp.* The table was covered with this huge red and white checkered tablecloth and before I knew it there were people who'd bellied up that I'd never seen but somehow knew and they just looked at me and looked, spoke Spanglish and smiled and laughed and drank and smoked, and I knew that these were Daddy's people because that's what he liked to do, and it made me sad that he'd never ever met these people who were so like him and would have loved him and they could have shared margaritas and tequila shots, blown smoke rings from their cigarettes up to the donkey piñatas strung from the ceiling, and his laughter'd join theirs, and the anger in his heart might go away.

And they were my people, too.

Daddy's brothers from the Mexican wife, with big dark eyes in one, and pale blue in the other, who spoke rapid fire and belly-laughed, who wanted to arm wrestle, who slapped me on the back and called me *hermanita*, and spiked my margarita with real stuff, just as their uncles had long ago when grandmother Josephine arrived and the party broke out where they cooked a dog named goat, danced and smoked all night, just like we would tonight on the 56th year anniversary. Sisters—*mi tias*—and a half-dozen *tias grande*, they had crazy long hair and swayed at the table, drinking doubles and ordering *sopapillas y mas totopos y salsa y mas queso para hermanita Lara,* and they cried and laughed and said it was my *quinceañera.* Jack was engulfed in the party that ensued, so he trotted along with the mariachis who played guitars over little amplifiers strapped to their waists, sloshed margaritas through mustaches, and it seemed like the room took flight, and it was like nothing I'd ever felt in my life, this inside joy bursting out, so it felt like home, only different.

Then came the food. Everything. Platters heaped with *refritos con queso*, *quacamolé* and bowlfuls of *molé* and rice and plantains, red, white and blue corn chips and buckets of bright red salsa this woman in an explosively red dress made with her hands table side, adjusting the heat for the brothers, making it sweet for the sisters, anything at all for hermanita y señor Jack. There came *suizas* and six kinds of enchiladas, fish tacos and these turkey burritos that were unbelievable. *Chili rellenos* swam the length of the table followed by *flautas* and the most wonderful flan drenched with honey, *peppinos ye tomatillos y salsa verde over puerco, pollo* cooked three ways and a whole lot of this soup with hominy in it that a brother called *pozolé*, which I'd later learn was Aztec for human flesh sacrificed to an angry god.

Papas fritas y camarones en frio, crema arroz and I must try the *coctel presidente*. *Huevos Motulenos, penachos con pavo* and a platter of *mole poblano con Guajolote*. *Carnitas* and *muy* different *sopas, pollo borracho* which came out under a sombrero.

The food bowled us over, made pigs of us, and finally, on a silver tray covered with a silver handled chaffing dish, the fire twinkling from below, decorated with embossed gauchos on horseback with long armed saguaros, set before us in the center of the table so that all went quiet, and Uncle Davey stood on the tabletop, tapped his margarita glass with a silver fork and cleared his throat.

"Today is ours *mi familia.* Our lost daughter, she's come home. The wound, the old hurt, it is healed. *Gracias, gracias mi madre y hermano. Gracias.*"

Tears fell when the lid was lifted. There, steaming before us on the silver platter, enough for every last soul in Guadalajara to have their fill, *cabrio para Hermanita con besos.*

Then, just before the serving, a silver framed photo is leaned to face me and the loud gaudy place ceases its spinning, is silent for the moment, the mariachis leaned guitars against the walls, cigarettes stubbed out and the flood of Spanish and English and all in between curses go quiet.

There, staring across the fifty some years, is my grandfather and grandmother, Buddy and Josephine, Daddy as a baby smiling between them. They look out at me with a question in their eyes, as if I know something they don't. It's outside a stone house, the photo, the sun low, the photographer's shadow thrown long against the dirt lawn.

17.

We are awakened by a blonde in cowboy boots, whose tongue-pink fingernails rap ever so gently on the screen door. *Yoo-hoo*, she sings, *anybody home?* Jack answers in his underwear, the bright blue day flung outside in every direction. She asks if we've seen Santa. The rattlesnake. He lives under the front door and comes out most mornings to soak in the sun on this the southern side. The ranch house owner whose site I rented the day after the election went south, she doesn't want us to be alarmed. *Santa* is not to pester us. She keeps a sixteen gauge shotgun in the main house. If the diamondback bothers us, we're to call her pronto—she'll take care of business. Six feet tall in boxers, Jack takes it all in through the screen door. The woman's lost her husband to melanoma. He was a golfer. Their children are grown, married, far from the Tucson ranch. The two horses neigh at her from a cinder block shed, hungry for the hay stacked just beyond the gate. The black one is Black Magic, the big white one, Geronimo, who's twenty nine years old. Have we lit the fire pit yet? There's lighter fluid in the black box.

In the one bedroom, I've taken the queen bed. Jack conked out on the three-unit couch in the main room, both of us stuffed to the gills with the Guadalajara fiesta. Noon light filters through white drapes dusty with desert, and there's a smell that makes me think of something I can't say. I hear them at the door, Jack and the Horse Woman, she's telling him the dog's name, the three cats, how she last saw the snake while watching game 7 of the World Series, the Cubs tied 6-6 with the Indians in Cleveland, when the rains came, and they rolled the tarps over the field and it had felt like time had frozen over for a while, don't you know, and she'd heard this sound, the dog growling—Wednesday night before last. She'd shot it, who she called Santa, with the sixteen, only it wouldn't die, kept dodging back into the hole under the front door where it lay no doubt this second, listening. The Cubs had won, 8-7, breaking the hundred-some year drought that had children hauling bottles of champagne to the graves of their parents, fulfilling the deathbed promises so many had made that should the Cubs ever win the Series, there'd be a party like there's no tomorrow on the patio of their final resting place.

"And I bought a bottle the very next day, and took it to my Harry's spot. The grass has grown in nice," she said, "And it was a jolt seeing my name there beside his."

She'd brought him a new box of balls, Titleist, his favorite, and his numero uno driver—a Big Bertha. They'd sipped champagne together and the old curse was broken and nothing, really nothing could ever take it away from them, even though he didn't really know, I mean, isn't it likely that the dead are dumb as doornails? Only the shot snake was back that afternoon, blood spattered from the birdshot she'd stung him with, and she'd known that it wasn't settled yet, something was on the radar. But what on earth could steal the ecstasy of the broken curse, the billygoat, black cat mojo undone at last, after two world wars, the invention of the car and rockets that blasted men to the moon, what could possibly undo the sweetness that had come to Cub fans after so much hardship and pain?

"It happened," the woman says. "The son of a bitch cast his shadow over us all, don't you know. Just Chicago's luck."

"The snake?" Jack asked.

"Santa baby's mine. I'll have his rattles. You been alive this last month? Do you know what's happened?"

Jack said, "I think so."

"Well good. That's good honey. Resist Satan and he will flee from you. There's another bottle of bubbly in there. You two have at it. Lord knows we need it."

"Thanks," Jack says.

I see her blonde hair shining. Her lizard skin boots. She's lost a husband, keeps a book on the counter called *The Night Sky for Dummies*. The phrase rings bell, though I don't know where. *Resist*—and he will flee from you.

"Thank you," the owner says, and I hear her boot heels crunch gravel up the drive until she's gone.

Today's the day we meet Uncle Davey for the drive up the Catalina Highway where the photograph I've brought of him as a sixteen-year-old was taken by grandmother Josie when she was twenty and about to have Daddy. Like Salt Lake, Tucson sits on this flat lake-like plain surrounded by mountains that rise to ten thousand feet and more, so it always feels like you're surrounded by a movie set backdrop. At night from the fire pit, you can see headlights crazy off the cliff highway that climbs up west to east, grazing the foothills up to the real peaks and Mount Lemmon where there's a ski resort and Summer Haven with its alpine timber mill that planed the lumber for Old Tucson. It's a good day, bright and clear, the air clean and dry and spring-like. We have juice at the bar looking out the picture window at Geronimo and Black Magic. They're in love, the owner said, and she's only waiting for the old stud to die before shipping the mare someplace east—New Hampshire, maybe, or Vermont. Last night's fiesta oozes from our skin, garlic and ancho and onion. The scent of corn tortilla.

"So what do you think about them? The Washers?"

Jack said, "I love them. What do you think?"

"It's so sad."

"There's not a sad bone in their bodies."

"I mean Daddy. That he's never met them. They're his blood. He's dead for them."

He passes a bowl of leftover *queso*, corn chips. Cold, I break two chips before breaking through.

"Bring your dad here and introduce them. That'd be a party." He looks at me, Jack, pulls the shirt up over his head, so it wedges behind his neck, his chest bare and white.

"He won't come."

"You got me here."

"So?"

For not the last time I see the red headed woodpecker, whacking the top of the arrow-shot saguaro, so the sound echoes off the barn where the horses glare at us to fork them some hay. It's true, Daddy won't come. It's poisoned for him, isn't it?

While Jack showers, I read *The Night Sky for Dummies*. Cassiopea is W shaped, or like an M, depending on whether it's winter or summer. Below the right hand point of the W in summer, Andromodae, a spiral galaxy—the farthest distant point in the physical universe visible to the naked eye. The best way to see it is to look away from it, see it with your peripheral vision evolved from the ancient days when our species had saber tooth tiger laying wait in the low light.

I listen for rattles.

He's stowed the phone, Jack has. But we both know there's a ticket waiting with his name on it at Greyhound, and if he doesn't take it soon, it'll be his butt. The thought of Mom and Dad comes to me, they miss me by now, wonder what's happened, why I haven't called. Maybe the Tripp woman's called. Saturday, maybe

I'm just sleeping in. Freshmen do that—sleep in. I've got one more day before they draw the line and check. For that matter, Jack's apeshit ma might have rattled their cage as well. Tonight, I'll check in. Tonight.

Jack's water stops, steam in little wisps through the just-cracked door. Out in the lot, Geronimo neighs, or is it Black Magic?

Towel-wrapped and dripping, Jack says, "Your turn."

Neither one of us is twenty-one. There's leftover everything in the fridge, champagne, who on earth could ever drink that? And the photo of Daddy as a baby, caught up between MaMa Josephine and Buddy, both dead now, on the other side.

And here we are, right in the middle of it. Me and a naked man. Anything could happen.

Anything at all. But we're who we are, and nothing does.

Daddy'll die. He'll fricking die.

"It's a coup, you know."

Uncle Davey's waiting for us at the intersection of Houghton Road and Catalina Highway, as if he's flown there with nothing but the hat on his head and a sackful of red-dyed pistachios. Jack gives him the front seat, shotgun, and the little man scoots the seat way up so Jack's got two feet of knee room. "That son-of-a-bitch Trumpet."

Wind from the open window gets in his bushy hair. Beardless, he's got on a blue shirt that's good with his eyes. Daddy's best color, blue.

"How's that?"

Davey sets the pistachios on the center console, slits the bag open with a fingernail. We pass just above the Saguaro National Park East, where our guest house is just now warming, a six-foot rattler, maybe, guarding the front door.

"The a son-of-a-bitch part? Or that it's a coup."

"Either," I say.

We've started up a mountainside covered with cactus, and before we know it the city's grown small beneath us, a toy city, far off Black Mountain on the other side of the valley overlooking the Mission San Xavier del Bac which is marked on all the maps as a must see destination.

"It's like this," Davey says, and holds one hand out the window so when he tilts it one way air whizzes upward, and the other way, down. He snaps his hand open and shut, open and shut. "That too much air on you son?"

Jack says, "No sir."

Polite Jack, my heart would hurt if anything ever happened to him. I don't know why I'm thinking that, but I am. What could happen to Jack?

"Can't grab hold of it, you see?

Davey snaps his hand open and shut a couple more times, smiles this wide smile, at me. "He's what we call a motor mouth, shootin' words at you so fast they go up one side and down the other. And truth is you can't *hear* that fast, nobody can. So you can't get ahold of his wind, old blowhard. Your grandfather would'a seen through his shit in a second."

"How did he die. Buddy."

"Heartbreak," Davey says.

We're hitting switchbacks now, rising, and it's starting for the world to look like that old black and white, the one that first caught my mind and turned it this way.

"Why was he heartbroken?"

Davey cracks the pistachios between his teeth, spits the colorful shells in the palm of his right hand, just like you know who does, shakes them so they rattle.

"You know the old story? The one about stranger comes to town. The only story, really."

The sage bundle on Mom's dash is fragrant—it's meant to cleanse the air, what Indians call *azilia*.

"Romeo & Juliet."

"Stranger comes to town."

He had a kind voice, musical, I could listen to him all day. Jack raises a brow in the rearview.

Who knew where we were headed?

"And the heartbreak part?"

"Darling," Davey says. "Have you ever *read* Romeo & Juliet?"

"I'm a freshman. I saw the movie. An African American and this skinny white girl. He was from the wrong side of the tracks."

"What else?"

"He was the stranger. They hurt themselves."

Davey points at a turn off just after a switchback where a sweeping panorama comes into view so that the world fans out, does backflips before our eyes.

"Take a right," he says. "Here."

I know the place, of course, from the photograph marked April '60 in the dusty Bible under Daddy's typing stand. A month pregnant, they'd made him in the west while still in love, and believing in that hopeful future he'd promised, where one day they'd own a house, a hacienda, with a garden and a veranda where the windowpanes blazed in the morning, and she could set up her easel and paint the magnificent light that falls on the ones in the photograph. They're on a blanket, five of my blood relatives, Uncle Davey's arms thrown up like Hercules in this very spot, there's the yucca, the view out over the big valley below.

I'm standing on it. Josephine says, *Say cheese.*

They're shirtless, the men, faces tanned leather. Octillo grows behind the blanket. A skinny boy sits apart from them, behind Aunt Ginger in her low cut suit, wearing Daddy's smile, a cigarette in his left hand. The one called Andy smiles on Davey's left, holding a pudgy arm, the yucca blooming, shirtless in April, morning sick already, Josephine. Buddy'd promised everything she'd ever wanted, Josephine, and she still believed that promised land was rolling down the pike, the cool breeze near the top of Mount Lemmon, the light wide open and you could see a hundred miles in all directions from up there, on that blanket. I've read where the baby's senses are soaked in the light and air of that place where they've been carried, that the born child will never be entirely happy in any other place.

The other one is of Buddy, posed, looking into the camera with the sun in his face. MaMa Josephine took the picture. He's in a white shirt, lit up, his left hand raised to his cheek, with the elbow resting on a jaunty knee. A handsome man, not smug, humble, looking back at her, a little question in his eye, the sky big as forever. On the back she's written: *This was taken on top of Mount Lemmon—what hopeful people look like. And the snow!*

To tell the truth, it reminds me of Utah. Upthrust mountain shining above valley below, in the heat of summer when you drive up there, plunge your hands to the wrists in it, like Daddy had when he first came, so he knew he'd come home, a mile high, seeing forever.

"I've seen this place before, Davey."

"Me, too," he tells me. "We come here to get away from hell."

"Where's hell?"

"Down there," he says and points.

Jack spreads the blanket, and we reenact the ancestral picnic, the remainder of the fiesta, the three of us. Thirty years from now, the photos will prove it happened.

Week thirteen of my first semester back at the U., I'm supposed to group study for a Building Communities project, only we've chosen to create a dystopia, all my groupies want to do is get high on a six-hitter bong and listen to Chance the Rapper and talk about what it will be like when we've all got iPhones wired into our heads and we don't have to go outside at all and who gives a shit about skinny jeans or dumbass homecoming dance. My roommates all pledged Tri Delt and got in, so now they say I can't come in the living room unless I know the secret sister password which they, bitches, keep secret. It's to the point where I hesitate to leave my room unless everyone's gone, which is more and more, and the big empty space ticks, and I can smell the remnants of rotten food in the rubbish chute, and it's hard to get out of bed, I don't want to really, what's wrong with me?

The truth is, well I've quit going to classes, mostly, no one knows but me. And my profs, I guess. In a month, when the grades come rolling in as I'm sure they will and Mom and Dad see my 1.9 GPA, after their jaws have dropped and they say the things they'll say, when I'm packing my "shit" and "getting the hell out" after Trumpet's first week of executive orders and then the second week, the Muslim ban and then the Dreamers, and soon after when the entirety of the *coup d'etat* is known and the world turns upside down for us all—the camps and shootings and martial law, when we fly this way again running for old Mexico in the ancestral tracks of Geronimo and the world is a different place altogether, I'll remember this moment, when Davey says to pull over and we get out and step onto the exact spot where so much that has been lost once stood, and I become part of the picture, twined with it all for good and ever.

After the photographs and prayers and *azilia*, when the blanket's been shook out and I've taken care to save three rocks—one for each of us—for luck, when Jack and I have had our last picture taken together, arm and arm with a mannish-looking saguaro at our backs, we hit the road back down to the valley, come upon the place where Houghton intersects Catalina Highway and drop Uncle Dave where we found him.

"How will you get home?" I ask.

He stands where maybe four feet tall, holding both palms up out in front of his chest. He raises his brows, a glint in his eye.

"*Ussen,*" he says. "*Ashagoteh.*" Mystery words.

Jack says. "Thank you."

He's back up front, shotgun, the seat moved back as far as it will go for his gangly legs. I'm smelling the sage, soaking in the light, the first tinges of hunger coming now in the late afternoon.

"Master Tripp. May your journey home be an uneventful one."

To me, he says, "*Mañana.* Back at Charro's. I want to show you something."

He's standing there when we drive off, smiling, his eyeglasses afire, flapping his arms, shadow wings.

18.

The snake is, of course, waiting for us at the front door. It's coiled on the welcome mat, a six-footer—I'm seriously not a snake person. Daddy got on this kick once of watching *True Grit* over and over. That's supposed to be Texarkana, he'd say, when Rooster and LaBoeuf galloped west, fourteen-year-old Mattie in tow, the full-blown snow-capped Rocky Mountains rearing before them. It was his first image of the West, Daddy's. One of his favorite parts was when Mattie got kicked into the snake pit, a whole writhing mass of rattlers on the floor. John Wayne as Rooster shinnied down on a rope that somehow came loose so there they were, sixty feet down, glittering eyes and forked tongues tasting them on the dank air. A wrist-thick one struck Mattie on the forearm, and Rooster shot its head off with his six gun. She cried out and it was up to goofy LaBoeuf—played by a real Arky, Glen Campbell—whose skull had been bashed in to haul them out, which he does, then dies. On the couch in the dark, after Mom had gone to bed, Daddy'd watch it over and over. Turns out that him and his cousin in Morrillton had once walked down from MaMa Stepwell's house to the movie theater on Main Street and watched it twice in a row when he was a kid—his first vision of the West, where he'd only just learned that he had been born, and he'd swore he'd go back, live there some day. In the dream, it was always me down in that hole, backing away from the snakes until my hand touches one, its jaws wide, fangs unfurled, Daddy falling, framed in light, my name loud from his mouth. I'd wake up screaming, sometimes Mom would be there, sometimes Daddy. *It's okay,* they'd be saying, *it's okay.*

Who on earth would name a snake Santa? It's *not* okay.

Laid out in the dirt as the snake's audience, the heeler dog, two cats, a woodpecker going off in the saguaro with the arrow through its crown. We could get the owner, have her blast the rattler to kingdom come with her sixteen gauge, so the gore would spatter the screen and doorknob and we'd touch it and see it and know it when we passed. We could do it ourselves with a rock, a stick, the pitchfork stuck into a hay bale down where Geronimo and Black Magic are neighing for us to hurry up and goddamn feed them the wedges we've been slipping through the gate the last few days. We could just use the back door and let the serpent be our guard. I don't know, what do you do when Santa's a rattlesnake?

Its rattles buzz, there in the sun, the light glinting off big diamonds that shine with golden scales. Its open mouth is like cotton, unhinged jaws, two clear fangs, a thin stream of venom leaking from each.

We walk right up, almost step on it. "*Jesus*," Jack says. "*Jesus*."

"Don't hurt it," what comes out of my mouth.

"Why?"

Through the front door window panes, I see our stuff: a backpack, inside of which was road food, Snickers bars and chocolate covered almonds, my emergency numbers, the pocket where Daddy'd stashed his pistol, once. For some reason the stove is covered with books, stacks on every burner, open the oven door, books and more books.

"Just don't."

"What then?"

I say, "Resist and he will flee from you." I don't know why.

"Don't be weird."

The heeler wags its tail, lays its snout between both front paws.

On the river, the ranger went over rules and regs, how if you fall in the river you should lay on your back and keep your legs up, so as not to tangle in a strainer; always pee in the stream so camp won't stink, and never go wandering near the water at night without a headlight and all your wits; don't touch petroglyphs or pick up pottery; if you see a snake, cover it with a bucket; be sure to tell everyone in camp what's under the bucket; when you break camp, pick up the bucket. Simple as that. Bad, bad medicine to hurt a snake. They ate rats and mice. The Hopi danced with them, called them brother. This was their space.

"Why did you come with me, Jack? What's this about?"

Jack says, "I don't know."

Except for the forked tongue, the snake's still as stone. It senses our heat, our underarm sweat, the aroma of our fear. What do I know about snakes? They can stand upright and some of them launch themselves from tall trees and glide on the wind. Their poison can be made into medicines that heal the sick, make the blind see again, raise the dead—some people believe its true. They crawl on the earth, connected to the ground. They shed skin and are reborn and so are worshiped as the cycle of life. Snake oil has fatty lipids in it that cures rheumatoid arthritis, which is in the lupus family—what MaMa Josephine had. The red spots on his forearm Daddy's passed to me, that's the sign you're afflicted. Maybe this snake was to be my medicine, a messenger, a herald of my life's change?

That's what I'm thinking, looking it eye to eye.

Behind us, the horses stomp. Geronimo chews a fence post. Way off in the distance, the Catalinas shimmer. Uncle Davey out there somewhere, appearing and disappearing. Mom and Dad are surely onto me by now. Daddy'd drive here, that's so him, save me from the snake pit, what a mess that would be.

Jack says, "Why do you think."

On the back porch is an empty hot tub with a drill on its stairs. Jack moves the drill and we sit, in the shade, facing a boxwood hedge like the one that used to mask the dinosaur window, all those little scraping tools and cement.

"You go first," I say.

"The snake's a sign. I read about it in Mr. Rose's class. Santa's a messenger and something big's about to change."

"That's why you're here?"

Jack picks up the drill. He says, "Yeah. I always wanted one of these."

"Why?"

"I don't know. Build a bird house or something. Haven't you ever wanted a drill?"

I say, "My whole life."

"All I do is talk on the phone. My bed at home has my butt indented in it. Yours, too, I bet. All of us. That's all we do. Follow each other on Facebook, snap each other, get jealous, feel left out. I'm lonely. Aren't you?"

"Right now?"

"I asked."

His eyes are blue, blue, and I don't believe—not even when he's so far gone that I can't even picture what he looks like, when I've forgot how he grinned at me that day on Mount Lemmon which overlooked forever, stuck a cactus bloom behind my ear and called me Rose of the desert—I don't believe there's ever been a moment so clear and real and *there*.

"I'm not lonely. Not now."

He said, "Me neither," clicked the trigger on the drill a few times then set it down. "Is that all?

"Yeah," I lied.

"Are you going back? To school, I mean" Jack said.

"Yeah."

"When?"

"Today. This afternoon."

"You'll take me. Won't you?"

"To the station."

"To the station."

"What about him?"

The air was clean and I could smell him, oranges and something else, snake scent from the rat hole under the welcome mat, sawdust, the crisp coolness of the air..

"Might be a her. We should get the owner. Cowgirl in the sand."

I said, "I'm going to miss you," and looked at his shoe, then his eye. I wonder what we looked like there, the dog, three cats, horses, and a rattler the length of a siphon hose examining us through slit eyes.

"I'm glad I came."

"Me, too."

"Come with me. We can drive back. Today, right now." Taller than Daddy, he touches my elbows, and just then the snake's rattles burst into a living salvo. A warning sign, danger near.

"Here's what we're going to do."

We walk, stroll together, really, to the cinder block shed where there's a white five-gallon bucket with a silver handle and a bridle bit rusting in the bottom. "You're going to take this and cover it up. We won't hurt it. We'll cover her up."

Black Magic sticks a muddy snout through the gate, yellow teeth coated over with scum.

The dog's followed us, is leaping into the air snapping teeth. Time seems to matter now, like if I understand the snake, everything will come clean.

We return to the front door of our guest house, where the rattlesnake has not moved.

Getting close enough to put a bucket over it seems risky. "You do it, Jack. You've totally got this."

Once Mom stepped on one's back while hiking, leapt three feet straight in the air, I swear.

Story is a copperhead once struck Daddy's Grandpa Si's wooden leg, and the old man would stomp, and the snake would strike. It's a family story.

He steps to the welcome mat, puts the bucket over the snake, scoots the whole thing out in the dirt far enough to open the screen door, which is open already, which means this serpent could have crawled right in and slept with us.

I say, "That was brave, Jack."

Out in the yard, the rattlesnake strikes the inside of the bucket, the buzz amplified and unnerving. Jack packs slowly, charges his phone. There's this pull between us, when I look at him, he turns away. What I'd give in ten years to have this back, the moment, Jack packing.

The whole time we can hear it out there—the snake striking the bucket.

19.

Three wimpled nuns stand in the blaring sun, each with an identical black suitcase at her feet. Their shoes are heavy black heels. The soles are worn. The sky is huge and blue, Picacho Peak off in the distance north where the cotton fields and pistachio orchards will have camps of the men and women who'd slipped across the border, who'd sipped the water stashed in stands of chokecherry and octillo, who'd burn night fires and tell stories of their people, how they'd first come to this place, seeking the eagle with a snake in its beak—the prophesied promised land that fell away to the sea. A wily raven and its shy mate hop the dusty parking lot, squalling at a stray bag of popcorn here, a wad of sunflower seeds there, sparrows and finches smashed on the windshields of buses bound north and west to California. I taste dust in the air, something else.

One of the nuns is dressed in fierce white, the other two in Bible black. Why? What's the difference between black and white? Looking back, they'll be what I remember, the nuns in their dark and light, how they glared at doves under the blue sky, the far off mountains with freak snow, saguaro, how utterly wide open we were then, nineteen-year-olds who'd road tripped from Utah, me and Jackson Tripp. I'll remember the nuns with their little black suitcases—full of snakes?—how it must have been for them to marry, so He was the groom and they the brides. The blue sky, cactus in the distance lifting hands in praise, throwing their man-shaped shadows. Or was it a cross?

The bus is gigantic, the driver in a uniform with his hair cut in a flat top so he looks military, sliding the nuns' suitcases into the underbelly. The windshield's blinding, like a blowtorch in broad daylight, and one of the nuns shades her eyes with a hand, so it looks like she's saluting. Inside, the radio chatters.

We hug. I smell him, Jack. He'd arrived for me in time for the feast. We'd selfied ourselves where Daddy's dwarf uncle had held arms up like a muscle man, a move Jack and I varied for a dozen shots.

He says, "Call me tonight. Come see me when you're home."

One by one, the nuns step up into the bus, disappear behind the shades, reclining seats where a baby cries, and someone has locked themselves in the potty.

"I will."

He says, "It was good crazy."

"You bet."

"Here." From nowhere, he pitches a fistful of flower petals into the air, scarlet, they flutter down on us, and I smell them and smell them still. And sometimes I've actually ached with the image of us on the shade side of the bus, red flowers falling all around, who I used to be.

Don't forget the snake, his last words.

Don't forget.

From high above in the Catalinas, on the far off peaks of snow-covered Mount Lemmon, where my grandmother once gazed down on this place, what surely must have seemed a wasteland compared to green Arkansas, where she carried my father on the day she photographed Buddy, the daddy Daddy'll never meet, how might we look from up there, on the flat dusty parking lot of the Greyhound Bus Terminal, with it's big dirt-stained sign? Could she have seen me and Jack in that moment before he boarded behind nuns, about to say goodbye forever, though we couldn't know that then, that this was our time. The three nuns with their severe black shoes and hard words spittling between them—how would we look to her from here? Would she know me as her son's daughter? What could she say from that other world to guide me or save me or keep me from ruin? And of Jack—without whom I'd have never made it here, six feet tall and brown as burlap. Would the rose petals flicker above our heads, and for a moment she'd say *no, don't let that boy go, don't.* There in the dead air on the bus's shade side, good crazy, he stepped up behind the stern-faced nuns and said goodbye. Waved his hand in little circles. From fifty years there to now, and fifty more, the circle between us making circles and those circles circles.

Would she know me as her own?

Will she ever let me go?

The bus retakes the highway. I watch till it's tiny, a toy, then gone.

On the way home, the Indians are still standing around the same park table as three days ago when we arrived. Have they moved? Are they alive? I wish I had something to give them, money, a baked turkey, *azilia*, I don't know what, and it comes to me to pray the way we do in lodge, just open up and say Tunkasila, please help those Indians and help me. And Jack. That's what I'm thinking as I drive down Broadway toward the guest house I'd rented on a credit card in Saguaro National Forest East Park, I mean, cactus can't make a forest, can it? A coyote stands frozen in the road just before the gate with its big Christmas wreath. It stands there looking at me with dark intelligent eyes. On the spot, I name him Jack. *Tunkasila*, be with Jack. Take care of him. Let him not be in trouble, too much. *Tunkasila*. The bright white bucket hasn't gone anywhere. It originally held Tide. I've heard there are tides in the desert, the sand dunes rising and falling. I fight the urge to look underneath, go inside and shower in the tiny shower, and imagine it curled under the nimbus of white, the warmth radiating under there, nothing to eat, no water, the shotgun lady vivid in its dreams. The moon would glow at night, the stars, the fanned out Milky Way. How that time when Daddy drove us to Croyden, Utah for *hanbleceye*—vision quest—a huge one swam out on the path to the fire pit where big Camille had told me to go and feed it some water, some scrambled eggs so Daddy wouldn't be hungry or thirsty. He was on the mountain. Evangeline had put him there, said *don't look at me, you are dead.* And I'd cried when she sang his death song, those high wails whistling sorrowful off the cliffs to the creek and cave with snow at its mouth in June. The llama tended the sheep, protected them from coyotes.

And then the snake had crawled out between me and the fire, and Daddy was dying—he had to have food and water.

"Brother rattlesnake," I'd said, and, at that moment, the thing had unhinged its jaws so both fangs dropped and this faint stream of venom shot from each. Then it swam away and that was that. Big Camille said the snake was my brother now, and the day I get the call that she is dead, White Plume the Lakota called her, I'll be thinking this, *brother rattlesnake, brother rattlesnake, brother rattlesnake*, the ghost dance my mind makes.

Jack's dishwater blond hair covers the tiny holes in the stall drain. Pinched between my fingers, I have the feeling somebody's here, that they've come in the open front door and wait for me in the next room by the couch. I shower, let the hot water run down my hair for a long time, light through the stained glass window, the smell of lavender and horse hair.

He's to Phoenix, by now, beginning to climb the Colorado Plateau. Soon Flagstaff and, before Page, Marble Canyon and Navajo Bridge, where the condor'd stretched out enormous white wings in the sun, the stripe faint on the underside.

Dressing to meet the old dwarf, it's the dog, the little heeler, snuck through the door and laying atop my bed. Bandit, the horse woman had said, or was it Bandito?

"Get," I say, and pet the thing. "Stay."

Inside, on the book-covered table, weighted by Korbell Brut, a note in Jack's hand:

I love you I forgot to say. You've got heart, you know, real heart.
I'll never forget up on that mountain. Me and you. I hope you find
it, what you're here for. Come home soon. J.

20.

The champagne bottle clinks against the seat belt buckle, a sound that gets under my teeth, only when I turn around to stop it the car swerves violently to the curb. I just miss a blue VW turning into traffic, the horn blaring. Calm down my heart. I sweat. Friday night's fiesta comes pouring out of my skin, the garlicky smell of my long gone self. That girl, the one who ate that food with those people, who drove across Glen Canyon and down into Arizona toward what she could not guess, who danced with a dwarf uncle in a room ceilinged by donkey piñatas, who'd photographed herself and that boy on the ancestral mountain, who'd run away from home, who'd thought to put the bucket over the rattlesnake, she no longer exists. I've washed her way. She's gone. *Adios.*

South Tucson, all the signs are in Spanish, so its like that time in Guatemala when I fell in love with trilled *Rs* and the aroma of scorched chilies and tortilla on a gust of earth-warmed air. Uncle Davey's outside Charro's in a three piece suit, a rolled up newspaper in one hand and a cigarillo in the other. He sees me coming, stands.

"*Buen Domingo*," he says. "Your boy get away?"

I say, "*Buen Domingo*," strange words, like when in Spain on *camino*, pilgrims always yelling *Buen Camino* at each other.

"*Ándale. Ándale.*" He points south with the newspaper, sights down it and pulls an imaginary trigger. "Toward *aeropuerto*. The Air Force base. *Camino Nosotros.*"

"*Si*," I say. I don't know why.

He smells like beer, Uncle Davey. Beer on a Sunday. I've never been in a car with a beer-breathed man on a Sunday, unless you count Daddy.

"Where are you taking me?"

The question seems legit. From here on, nothing's planned. "You'll know when we get there, sweets. Big time. *Por favor.*"

He turns the radio on, a Mexican station with drums and the word *corazon* said over and over. He lets the seat back, kicks his little legs out and reclines. Something has ended and something else begun. Drive south, he said. That's what we do, drive south.

Pima County Fairgrounds, where Uncle has me park next to a stockyard with a Volkswagen high pile of cow manure, features a billboard announcing Sunday Night Wrestling under a graffiti painting of The Angel of Sorrow, who, according to Uncle Davey, was once famous for biting the heads off live chickens. Before each match, he'd chomp one, so the headless body'd run around doing backflips and you could see the moving beak clenched between his teeth. Uncle Davey back doors us into what must have once been the Angel's dressing room, and there he is, himself, in a chair with an enormous black wing hanging from either shoulder, reading poetry of all things, Baudelaire's *Les fleurs du mal* with this far-off bongo music playing from a transistor radio. Unlike his photograph, which shows a wild man with a chicken head stuck out of his mouth and a whole lot of blood running chin to chest—EATS CHICKEN ALIVE writ underneath in big white letters—this Angel seems perfectly sane there in his reading chair, the light shining on the lenses of his glass so his eyes sort of blazed the way the Greyhound bus's windshield had when the nuns boarded and Jack swiped back a tear and so did I. Uncle Davey makes me walk in front. I have not one idea why we're here.

The room was plain Jane, neither big nor small, hot nor cold. There was a smell, incense or sage, maybe. Cedar? Pot?

Angel looks up from his book, regards me through reading glasses. He tilts his head one way, then the other. His dyed blond hair is thin on top, the rest tied back in a pony tail. "Good afternoon. Lord Fontelbury will introduce his guest?"

"Buddy's granddaughter. Lara, meet Otto. The Angel of Sorrow. I left a message."

"So you did."

A rodeo poster hangs over a dilapidated couch, some soup cans in a cardboard box. For some reason I picture our basement back home, dark, all Daddy's river gear and broken oars and the duck hunting waders that look like a man standing in the corner, the little hole to who-knows-where with a board thrown over it.

"*Lara*." He says my name, then says it again, stretching the A's. "That's a name for a Russian princess who's beautiful and falls in love with a poet and they make love passionately in the ice palace before revolution and then they part and die. I'm Otto. That's *toot* inside out. A pleasure." Angel bows. Both his knees crack.

"Nice to meet you," I say.

"Your uncle once wore the belt," Angel says. "He won't tell you that, but he did. Where are you from?"

Davey says, "Utah. She's Buddy's granddaughter. You have something of hers in your keeping."

Angel snaps the book shut. "I can see in your eye that you're not one of *them*." There's a smell, like the lizard tank at Hogel zoo.

I say, "My Dad's a historian," for some reason.

Angel eyes me through reading glasses. Shirtless, his belly hangs like a feed sack. "Your father has studied the affairs of men?"

"Mountain Meadows," I say. "The Massacre."

Otto says *hum*. This close I can see he's missing teeth, his molars.

"I once wrestled the Mormon Assassin. He could say the ABCs backward."

"She's been here since Friday. It was free beer for vets at Charro's. Today's her last day. She's leaving tonight. It's time."

The two men pass looks.

At the far door, just as he disappears, a deep baritone, *Laura's Theme*, cascades away and we are alone with *Les fleurs du mal*, the rodeo poster, a smell from another world.

"How'd he get his name? Angel of Sorrow."

Davey takes a seat on the couch, the colorful rodeo behind his back. "Everybody has to be called something,"

The Angel returns with a box giftwrapped with a poster from a wrestling match that pitted the Fabulous Kangaroos against El Diablo and Little Lord Fontelbury.

"Here," he said. "Don't open it till you're gone. Way gone," he says. "I might change my mind and want it back." He eyes Uncle Davey. "And who would stop me from that?"

Uncle Davey straightens, and I see in his eye that look I've seen on Daddy's face a thousand times, how he'd look at me right this second, if he could see me. How its flashing through his brain to rip your rompers, to lay you low, all the ways of putting violence into words.

"Thanks, Otto." He holds up his hand and the two men shake.

"Will there be anything else?"

"That's it," Davey says.

"Well good day then."

I say "Good day," take the gift in my right hand, which trembles a little. "I won't open it until we're gone."

He nods. "*Way* gone. I see him in you."

"Who?"

"Ask your uncle," he says. "Be wise."

21.

Trash lines the ditches built for a flood that must have evaporated in another lifetime, the place is so dry. No grass, weeds, scraggly bush hither and thither, the reservation is home to a kind of Indian whose name I can't say. I'm low on gas, just over an eighth, and Davey's rolled his window down so the wind's in his hair, making his hand into a little airplane—zoom up, zoom down. *Ave Maria*, a sign says, *Casa de Inspiración*, and I swear I see sparks, little meteors, moments of white hot light, that's how it starts, just when the white bell tower comes in view.

We pass a little cemetery with a sign that says *no photographs,* and they're dancing out there, under a full moon, the old ones gathering to meet me, for my arrival, they have come and started the ancestral wine dance, the Tohono O'odham, *Bac* in another tongue, their eyes glint as chert in starlight, as Vishnu Schist does at the bottom of the Grand Canyon down past Lava Falls, where it fans out over four-billion years—these eyes are like that stone, impervious, forever. There's a drumbeat and I sense fire, somewhere near the ceremonial fire is burning, and its keeper had learned from it of my coming, my escort in a black mask, there is a stool at the foot of the wooden man, the virgin herself revealed, the long ago uttered prayer and the gift that accompanied it, they have been received, the mediation has taken place, all be joyful. I don't know how all this comes to me, passing the cemetery gate toward a site that I will learn has been sacred refuge across space and time for so many, their stone eyes on me, their spirits smiling, it is good news that I have come to this place, they have seen me before, how is it with the child? Josephina, how goes it with *el niño la navidad?*

The outer gate, flung wide open, the sanctuary doors, open wide, the first station of the cross where I'll see the first sign of the closing circle and my part in all of this, open. Many candles burn, they flicker out in all directions, faces of painted saints crazed-eyed on the walls, real hair flowing from the scalps. High above the far-away altar, he looks straight into my heart, San Xavier, a tall thin man with hard eyes. He hangs there above the desert altar—*my sister, come home,* I'll never quit seeing him now.

It's raining on the foothills now where Mama and Daddy walk, the bark on the gamble oak slick and dark, he's carrying sage, my father, matches, cedar, he'll burn it at the foot of the mountain mahogany somebody's shot with a shotgun, before I was born, it came back, it kept trying, like Geronimo, he told me once, never quit trying. He'll hold a match to the white sage wrapped by Bill Bolan, a holy man on his way to Rosebud, South Dakota, Lakota Territory, Crow Dog's Paradise where the men pierce themselves and hang from a cottonwood tree until their flesh rips free and the sacrifice is complete, gathered in a holy bundle and pulled into the highest branches where the embodiment of a man and a woman colored by Indian children on butcher paper, flutter in the blast furnace heat. Smoke will curl from the tree base and they will pray, both of them in plain words—*Tunkasila, thank you for the blessings of this world. Thank you for my family, my daughter, my wife, my husband, my Lara. Be with us and help us walk in a good way. Thank you for all those who've given love, who've breathed prayer, who helped get us to this place.* He'll light the cedar, the sweet grass. He'll touch the tree, and she'll *say thank you for this rain. Be with Lara. Let her know we love her, we miss her. Keep her safe. Let her call.* A magpie will yammer from the rabbit brush, the dog will bark, another family will appear where the trail tops out. They'll start down the shadow side of the mountain where red sandstone was quarried once, big flat wedges the size of cars, *il pluet,* Daddy'll say and walk to the rock I jumped to him from as a girl, his arms wide, the great blue salt lake behind him, so it seemed I leapt into forever, the space between us more than a breath.

Just inside the thrown open doors, standing in the exact spot my grandmother Josephine once stood, gazing into the deep where candlelight flickers, the spirit world takes breath to greet me.

The saint's eyes see us through.

Painted on the white plaster of the loft wall, a lyre, the sign I was born under, named for Orpheus who'd returned to the underworld for his love, Eurydice, only he'd turned around to make sure she followed, and he lost her there, and wept and cried and played ever so sadly on the instrument so that the nymphs tore him and it to pieces, flung him into the sky to be the sign I was born under. Directly opposite the loft wall, the shining length of an arm, a feathered fountain pen writing in an open book. That would be the sign for Daddy, him and his history, how this all comes to be seen from that place those who come after will inhabit. I'll learn that this place and all of its paintings had fallen into ruin, water damaged and time worn, so when Mama Josephine stood here in my tracks, the signs were faded, invisible to her and everyone else until the great restoration when the images were coaxed back to life for the living. The lyre and the fountain pen, the open book—very much here now, very much alive. The white dove of the desert is reborn.

The pews have been refinished. They shine.

High above the far altar, San Xavier calls in the language without words, what the heart understands. And I'm not alone. I don't feel alone. There are souls here with me now. I know this. I know.

The aisle falls just slightly and I'm walking slow, the ceiling spinning ever upward, angels and doves, a woman whose head is shrouded in light, a nimbus, and above her the light itself. They were invisible to her, the lyre and the fountain pen writing in an open book. Before the restoration, she couldn't see them there, but felt them nonetheless, as I feel her now. Eyes see me with my left hand on a pew on the east wing of the cross, they see me as I see the Indian nativity with its three candles burning through the ages.

The last time I saw MaMa alive I was three and don't remember. Daddy'd driven us to Florida that June for Poppy's birthday, down in Melbourne Beach where Mom photographed me running from a wave, a big breaker, this smile on my face and the curved world of ocean behind us. We'd driven up the coast of Georgia and South Carolina, I can follow the trail on a map, Skidaway Beach where we camped and Mom'd kicked Dad in the head for snoring. To Cape Lookout Cabin Number Seven, the Alger Willis Fish Camp, dunes of wavy sea oats and those men who spoke the funny language and people on the mainland buried loved ones in their front yards, made pathways to the carved stones out of sea shells. And then Arkansas where we'd lived once in a dream house with a barn and loft we'd once climbed into at night with that strange man who'd lost his daughter, and Daddy'd flipped the lights on and we'd stood at the open loft door, Mom and the dead girl's mother invisible beneath us. And finally to Lonoke and the Harvells and Mom Dee had met us at our hotel, and I swam with my cousin, Trace's son, and Mom had set up her camera just outside of the gazebo where we were arranged. O.W., who's forgotten me now, he's smiling, Dougie at his side and Daddy at his back with his arm around Mom—she'd had to run from the tripod twice to beat the flash. There's Trace, who's got O.W. in her face, his big limbs and shoulders. I'm in Mom Dee's lap, her with the green eyes and sweet smile on her movie star lips, a pink blazer with a low cut shirt beneath—a flower blooming on her breast. In a Pooh swimsuit with a bag of open corn chips flat on the table in front, there's me, waving, one hand held up before us all, fingers splayed, a little fear in my eyes, maybe, the not knowing. Beside me, Josephine, pale, her hair not washed, not ready at all for this moment. She summoned a smile, a real one from her heart, her earth eyes wide. There we are framed beneath glass on the mantle of the house I grew up in, where I learned to walk and say ABCs, and the ungodly mess I made of my first cellphone, ourselves looking out at ourselves from the gazebo. Daddy's face is burned from the beach. He'd sit under that very gazebo to write her elegy, or was it eulogy, I always get them mixed. The last time we were photographed together, I remember none of it, not one bit, but it happened, I was there, and it wasn't a dream. I know now she'd prayed for this, on that faraway birthday when she turned twenty, already in her ninth month—she was my age exactly, a girl, far from home, alone, in trouble.

She'd looked into the face of the saint and he'd beckoned her. There was the Indian nativity, a manger in the desert with the huge blazing star shining down, flickering, the three candles lighting the faces, the chert-eyed Madonna who the baby crowned in light reaches for, the father's braid hanging between them, a saguaro lifts arms and the animals have come—the rattlesnake, coyote, an owl blurs the boundary between sky and earth.

The boy would be born on Christmas. He'd never see the father on this side. There would be blood. Great danger. Deceit, betrayal, violence, murder even, hidden in the light and dark tones beneath the gazebo, how we smiled, and I raised my hands as a three-year-old to wave and acknowledge who I am now, Floradee beside me, Mama Josephine, her prayer on the spot where I stand answered, finally, with my coming, she sees me from beyond the manger, in the star-shadow cast by the saguaro, the glowing cross reflected in the eyes of the rattlesnake, the coyote, the owl that blurs the boundary between sky and earth, she soars on owl's wings—isn't that what was said?

Beside me a man is praying. He is saying *thank you, oh thank you*. He means it. I can tell. He means it with his whole heart. He has loved someone deeply and that person has somehow been helped, there has been intercession. Prayer has been heard. I stand there with my great uncle. We are alone before the Indian nativity. He reaches me three candles, and the three candles join the three Josephine set fifty-six years earlier. We light the new from the old. The fire is the same fire. I'm saying *thank you, oh thank you*. I can tell by my voice that I mean it—with my whole heart.

Mother, holy, I thank you.

Outside, the air radiates with goodness. As if I've left all that does not serve me at the altar beneath the hard eyed saint, the candles lit and guttering this second on the nativity that sews the rivet between earths. From the front door a pathway winds up a hilltop where many are walking, up and up and up, a few carrying bundles of flowers. It's the path I'm meant to walk, up the hill where women carry flowers, that's my way, how I'm supposed to go. "You were right to bring me here, Davey. How did you know?"

In the plaza Indian families cook frybread over charcoal fires, pounding the dough one hand to the other, the smaller of them pushing toy trucks in the dirt, some rising, and I can smell it from here, the frybread. I'm hungry somewhere deep inside, as if I've fasted the four days of vision quest, and now am being led to the promised feast.

Not yet. In time.

"It's Sunday," Davy says. "We used to all go to church on Sunday."

The women bearing flowers have all disappeared on the trail that winds up the hillside, the only hill on the valley floor as far as I can see until the Catalinas, snowy Mount Lemmon and Summerhaven.

"I walked up there with her. That other time."

"Who?"

He's taken my hand, Davey, and that's okay. The rise is gentle, moves from left to right, the right way, three-hundred-and sixty-degrees around the hill three times from the base to the grotto.

"Your grandmother. Josephine. It was her birthday. I brought her here."

"Why?"

"She needed to pray at a church. That's what she said. That she needed to pray at a church."

Turning west, old Mexico is beyond the black mountain, then north again where the sage and cedar smoke twist into the sky with Mama and Daddy's words, let them know I'm well.

"I don't remember her. My grandmother. Was she nice?"

East again, ancestral road home. South, the black mountain, down walk the flowery women, faces tear-streaked, why?

"An angel. Buddy hit the jackpot. He never deserved such as her."

"And where is he?"

"Your grandfather is incommunicado. It's just around this corner."

West, for the third time, Picacho Peak, Phoenix, the Pariah Plateau, Jack somewhere heading home, and then north, the mountains again, the vision my grandfather'd seen from a prison yard while his young wife hemorrhaged, her son and his born on a river of blood, she the boat that ferried him across. Had he prayed, who never deserved such as her. In this world, who deserves anything at all?

Me?

We turn the corner of the hill's top, north facing, so the sun pours into a barred grotto where flowers are piled on thousands and thousands of photos and poetry and scarves and every sort of gift and plea imaginable. A plaque tells how the sacred virgin appeared here, that this is holy ground. Show respect. Do not to smoke. Alcohol is forbidden except as offering.

"You came *here*?"

Davey says, "Yes. Right here."

"On her birthday?"

The light just pours and pours, the plaque letters burning, the words on fire— *please intercede for us.* Full daylight, the moon and sun both visible now, rain in Utah, *il pluet.* A pair of ring-necked doves zing over, the *ta ta ta* of their wings reverberates in the sacred cave.

In my front pocket, the phone rings that second, 901 area code, Daddy.

"She was twenty. That day. Can you imagine being twenty?"

I say, "Yeah, Davey. I can."

Beneath the burning words, as if placed there for me alone to find that second, a ground shrine says *Here Appeared the Blessed Virgin who Intercedes For Us With Christ The King.*

They might have been real pearls, the earrings. They glittered, set in silver at the foot of the plaque.

Dear Mary, please speak to Him for us.

Between my finger and my thumb, the clasps link the two into one. No one has to tell me anything ever again. That these—this—belonged to one who came like me, breathing prayer. The gift and the gifted.

"Damn," Davey's saying. "*Damn, damn, damn.*"

I lift the earrings to my lips, kiss them, lay them be. There's the aroma rising from the charcoal pits below, food for the hungry, the promised feast at the end of her wanderings.

Thank you. Thank you. Thank you.

22.

Uncle Davey decides to show me my grandfather's grave. Back in South Tucson, we find Saint Monica Catholic Church and South Lawn Cemetery which is really mostly bare dirt and plastic flowers laid at stones that glare from the distance, so that someone passing above in an airplane descending to the airport two miles south might mistake them for swimming pools, or so Davey says, a thought too odd for me this Sunday, the frybread good in my stomach, Mother's words deep inside my heart's heart. I don't know why. I'm no Catholic. Nor have I ever really even been to church, except for the times with Poppy, when I'd follow him up to the altar, take the sacrament, the bread and bitter wine, and this one time the priest scowled and said, "Is she a member of the flock?" And Poppy'd said, "You goddamn right," and the priest turned white, and his hands shook as he administered the body and blood.

The wrought iron gate turns loose an awful squeal when Davey pushes it open, and why I've brought champagne into the cemetery, god knows—maybe I heard about it because of all the Cubs fans who'd sworn to the parents and grandparents and great grand parents that should the Cubbies ever win a series, they'd bring bubbly to their graves and have a bygod party—why not? And it happened, for reals. Such happiness as has never been seen in Chicago, and the whole country, and then Trumpet had to blare his way into office and ruin every damn thing. I'm sorry, they'd say. I didn't vote for the s.o.b. Not my president. Resist. Stop your spinning down there, Ma. I brought the champagne. Okay?

Sunday afternoon in the cemetery...

Sunday afternoon in the cemetery where the father Daddy never met lay buried. The bottle's slippery, grease from the frybread on both hands, under my nails, long unpainted, chewed, what will become of me?

The tombstones that flyers mistake for swimming pools are strung with rosary, cross, Easter bunnies and Halloween scarecrows, plastic flowers faded by the sun, whiskey bottles, tobacco, a *Playboy Magazine* on one, the surnames multiplied many times over for these Catholics—the Quinns and Bergers, Franklins and Tyndals, Triolo and Hernandez and Molinas. The stray Mendoza. Cargo planes roar overhead landing and lifting off from the airport across the way, Tucson International, and further east, Davis-Mothan Air Force Base where Buddy was stationed before transferring to JVille, Arkansas where he was twenty-one and looked like James Dean, his hair swept back and teeth white as the gleaming plaster of Mission San Xavier, and Josephine had fallen for him and his white lies. They'd eloped and, depending on who was telling the story, were either married by a sleepy justice somewhere in the big heart of Texas, or in Danville with Josie's people, where he'd worn a uniform and I have a photo of both of them holding the knife to cut cake. The braided stories twine and intertwine and nobody will ever know what really happened, will they? There was bad blood. A child was taken. And from that child, me. The answer to the question of what really happened—me?

"Here," Davey says. "Just over there."

In my memory, he'll always wear the three-piece suit, blue-eyed, his hair combed back and oiled, bright eyes, Daddy's widow's peak. I see myself in him, standing at his brother's grave.

Pr. William "Buddy" Washer

August 18, 1937-September 19, 2005

U.S. Air Force Korea, Vietnam

father, son, brother, husband, grandfather

gone, not forgotten

Davey sobs. It's not something I expect. He says, "I brought her. Buddy. Just like I said I would. She's got the gift. Say hello."

He says *hello,* Davey says.

A long handled spatula leans against the silver stone with its dark carved letters in Times New Roman, red dirt blown into the crevices. He wipes it clean with a white handkerchief which he tri-folds, returns to his pocket. He says, "We been to the church."

He says you look like your grandmother.

"How do you know?"

Davey says, "I just do. He made me promise. To bring your daddy here."

His bones are down there. His hair. His DNA, mine. And with a shock I see that he's not alone, that beside him lies his mother, Katherine Violet Tremaine Wash, and beside her, a sister, my great aunt. And over there a child with a little lamb stone, there's a whole slew of Washers here—my people?

"Promise what. To bring *me*?

Doesn't matter, he says. *You're here. Now. Tell me about yourself young lady. How is your father. Why idn't he with you?*

Davey sits cross-legged in the dirt beside his brother's tombstone. *Have a seat. Make yourself at home.*

I say, "Hello. My name is Lara Harvell."

You look like her. You brought a bottle.

"I've heard that before. That I look like her. It's what Daddy says."

Go on. Open it. This is happy time.

"My father. Daddy's in Salt Lake. With Mom."

The first word he ever learned was Da. Da, da, da, he said, it drove Josie crazy. That he said da before ma.

"They don't know I've come. That I'm here." I've never opened a bottle of champagne, the act is beyond me. I pass the bottle, warm from the car and slippery with frybread grease to Davey, who makes it explode, a froth of sweet-smelling fizz spewing from the mouth. "I needed to get away."

Good. Good, good, good. Some for me, Davey boy.

Davy sloshes the stone, the name, and that second a wind comes up, just blows in from the west desert right through my bones. And what happens next, and what happens after that, I'll try to tell my father, and years later, the children, a son, my love, but I'll never get it right, not ever, really.

Girl.

"That's you," Davey says.

I say, "Yes."

You've come home.

"My home's in Salt Lake. I go to college there."

We've waited for you. A long time.

It's Violet's voice, I know, my grandmother, who'd gazed through MaMa Josephine into the grandson that would be stolen from her, a theft she cursed until the day she died, and to now, even. I know this though no one's ever told me.

"Mama," Davey says.

You're ours now. Don't forget that.

There's the voice of the sister, of the little lamb child calling for its mother, others, they twine and intertwine, and the champagne bottle is passed and passed until its in my hands. The wind stops. It's quiet.

Your father?

I pour what's left at his feet, Buddy's.

"He's in history. He talks about Geronimo. How he always wanted to go home. From Oklahoma."

Can you bring him here? To this spot?

I say, "I'm here."

For him?

"For what?"

You don't know?

"How could I?"

He promised to come here. To meet the family. To right that old wrong. He belongs to us. He promised. I can't go until his word is kept. Comprendé?

Davey makes the sign of the cross on his chest, shuts eyes, he's saying "Hail Mary, full of grace."

I say, "I am his word."

And the one comes after you. It's mine, too.

"Buddy," Davey says. "Buddy."

Where is my son?

There is silence. Nothing but a jet lifting east from the air base, about to break the sound barrier. Light on the carved stones. *I am here. I am his word.*

Fine. Give him this. And we're even.

Davey unhooks the dog tags from the stone, slings them in an arc to me, so the sun catches the front and the back, the silver chain. His name, rank, serial number.

"Put them on," the old dwarf says.

Around my neck, sun-warmed, light, they tink.

Done, the disembodied voice says, and is no more.

The crooked crosses lean as far as I can see. A jet breaks the sound barrier over at Davis-Mothan, the thunder beings burn off over the Santa Catalinas crisscrossed trails, double helix DNAing north.

We leave the bottle on the stone, push through the squalling gate, drive away and don't look back. Davey's got business at Charro's—can I drop him there, it's good that I have come.

"What'll you do now?" he asks.

Picacho Peak is shadowed in the distance. I know she looked there—maybe he did too. We are mixed with what we see, the white dove in the desert, cactus, star. I was born under a full moon, I tell Davey. Tomorrow's full moon.

"Wolf," he says.

"All the women in the birthing center were screaming bloody murder, threatening castration of anything with a dick.

Davey smiles, sing-songs "*Frosty Castrado.*"

"Mom too, she screamed. Daddy was there. He hummed and walked me down the hall where they drew blood. He likes to tell that story. How they poked my heel and I screamed and it was like a knife going through him, my scream."

"Mine was a waning moon—a getting smaller moon." He's smiling still, shakes my hand, then hugs me over the stick shift. "You're welcome anytime. We'll roast the goat."

"What about that?" Between us, on the center console, the gift wrapped in a wrestling poster from when Davey was on the card, when he was Little Lord Fontelbury.

"Not now. Wait."

"Till I'm *way* gone."

"Yeah," he says, opens the door and hops out. "We love you, sis."

Here comes a whole troupe of wrestlers in costume, boozy, cigarettes hanging from the sides of their mouths, the colorful coterie come marching off the walls of Charro's, come walking up the sidewalk, singing "Lord forgive us and protect us, we've been drinking whiskey for breakfast." The rear guard, The Angel of Sorrow. Otto waves at me, smiles.

"I love you, too."

Uncle Davey holds his index finger to his lips, says "*Shhh, sugar.*"

He steps up into the revelry, the dwarves and giants and masked men, The Angel of Sorrow and Tunnel of Love, they go on marching, I don't know where. He turns to wave bye, blows a kiss. They parade past the plasma center, the trailer park with its busted out screens, maybe even the same one that Buddy dove up beside all those years ago, when he'd promised Josephine a mansion, that they were all rich. When the car radiator'd overheated and the Washers came walking out, the old dwarf young then hopping through the screen, spurting the radiator off with a water hose. Where Josephine had spent her first two weeks, pregnant already with Daddy.

Another world ago.

"Lord Forgive us and Protect Us," bleeds into "When the Saints Go Marching In." A horn is blowing, I'm swearing to god.

They sing and go on singing and disappear.

All the way home, the Subaru is sweet with his champagne breath.

Later, it'll all swirl together, the Mission San Xavier del Bac and the cemetery, the voices of the dead and the living, shining Mount Lemmon and the Catalina Highway. Snake Woman will be there with a sixteen gauge, coyote slinking into the shadows, me and Jack dancing the *bachata* under a ceiling festooned with donkey piñatas. All the wrought iron gates will scream hallelujah, and a parade of angel-headed freaks will beckon me to follow. The rattlesnake will unhinge its jaws, and I'll see a world that could have been.

And there's one more thing.

After we'd climbed down from the grotto where Blessed Mother had appeared, I'd gone to the bathroom, and inside the stall, lying on the concrete was a sticker someone had dropped. On it, a black diagram, a circular maze the size of a silver dollar, the black lines sharp against the white, a maze of circles swimming to the center where there was a black dot out of which all else swirled. I'd later learn that it was two things at once: the circle maze with the black heart was a fertility symbol of the Tohono O'odham, a sign of gestation, *enceinte*, fecund with life—a vulva. And the symbol was a kiva, a place of prayer, the holy site of mediation between heaven and earth. At the kiva mouth, the shape of a man, the maze is of his making. A child at the kiva mouth, hauling the prayers of this earth to father sky. A child comes forth from the vulva, from the tomb of the womb. Both things at once. Magic. If you can believe this you can believe anything at all.

There in my hand, for a moment—and for *only* a moment—it all made sense, the whole story, all of us, everything. And then it was just a drawing, black on white. But I've held onto that piece of paper, that sticker. For my whole life I've kept it to remind me of the vision. And maybe one day I'll see through it again, to the other side, the place where all makes sense.

Part 3

23.

Geronimo and Black Magic neigh in unison while I pack up my bags. Bright Monday morning, the sun shines on the crown of the saguaro with the arrow shot through a good foot of its flesh. The heeler dog I've named Sam leaps at my side and there are flowers blooming yellow and orange on the south side of the barn. With the pitchfork leaned there by snake lady for this very purpose, I fork two thick wedges of hay over the gate, and the horses munch it between yellow teeth, nodding big muddy heads, standing on heaps of their own manure. Beyond the fenced lot, the Saguaro National Park reaches up into the foothills where horse trails wind visibly. The dog leaps happily at my side. What kind of name is Geronimo for a horse? Black Magic? I fork them more hay, straight onto the mud and manure where they stand, they live in beauty, they stand on mud and shit. The two are the same. Had I spoken to my dead grandfather? His mother, Vi? Had a baby cried? Does the desert sharpen one's senses until the dead speak on its dry breath? Mom? Dad? You'd like it here. The light is good. The mountains and the sky. It's a day for going places. The full super Wolf moon, pulling everything to kingdom come. High tide, the desert alive, rippling. November, Josephine's 76th birthday soon.

She was my age way back when this all started. The earrings were hers, I know. Her gift. Our gift.

The last thing I do before driving out of the city where my father was born, but doesn't remember, after I've checked the tires and made a turkey sandwich with mayo and cucumbers the way I like it, when I've filled water bottles and given some to Sam and the evil cats, when Geronimo and Black Magic have each had five sugar cubes apiece and a red-headed woodpecker is whacking hell out of the arrow-shot cactus, I stand before the ghost-white bucket to make peace with my snake brother.

"Brother," I say, knock three times on the bottom of the bucket.

Don't forget the snake, Jack had said. What of him? Is he home yet? Would he think of me? What would he tell his mother? How would our story get told? Don't forget the snake.

I knock again. "Brother," I say.

The woodpecker's going to town—*whacka, whacka, whack*. Some birds eat snakes, wasn't that how Mexico City was found, a bird with a snake in its beak? Perched on a cactus, an eagle eating a rattlesnake.

I knock on the hollow bucket one last time, kick it over and leap back, trying for all I'm worth to stay air-bound.

Only there's nothing there. The rattlesnake is gone.

Back under the front door? Coiled beneath the passenger seat in the Subaru? Tasting the yellow flowers with its forked tongue? I'll never know. But like so much else from this trip, I'll think about it for a long, long time, knowing that he could reveal himself anyplace, anytime.

Don't forget the snake.

Coyote Jack eyes me on the way out, thinking God knows what.

Daddy's beat up atlas, the one that's duct-taped together and has red lines and circles drawn on all the pages of the states we've ever visited, and even on the big picture of the whole United States up front, a red line magic-markered west from Greensboro, North Carolina across Tennessee to St. Louis and Kansas City, north toward Lincoln, Nebraska, Cheyenne to big circled Rawlins—home of the ancestral rodeo that marked their arrival west, down to Salt Lake City with its big blue lake in plain sight of where I was born, my *omphalos*, the center of my world.

Arkansas and Arizona face each other, one on the right, one on the left, and before I know it I'm on the very highway that connects the two, old Highway 10 past South Tucson and the Davis-Mothan Air Force Base in sight of Buddy Washer's grave, south and east—the exact road Josephine escaped with her firstborn a half century ago, the rest is history.

My hands smell like gasoline from the 7-11 pump where I paid with a credit card Mom and Dad would trace. The radio's on, a Mexican station, the words *mi corazon y tu?* Jack's left his blue water bottle in the passenger floorboard, and I wonder what else of his is left behind, where he is now, what he's doing, how my bitchy roommates are getting by. Classes today—Tai Chi, Wilderness Training,

Building the Perfect Community. To my left, rising with gleaming snow on its back, Wild Horse Mountain. I pass a sign that says Visit Colossal Cave, and I wonder if Josephine ever went there when Buddy'd drive her down to the Tombstone Ranch, one of the only true things he'd ever told her about his family, how his great, great something grandfather had been sheriff there in its heyday, all the Geronimo business about running from General Crook, the last wild, free Indians left in the continental U.S. And Katy Tremaine had been very real, as I've heard it. They met, Josephine and Katy, the fireplace story, how the kids all climbed up to hide because Geronimo'd kidnapped a white girl, skinned her head to toe, made a medicine pouch he always wore around his neck. She'd climbed down and saw them out under the cottonwood where Daddy's birth sack is buried, the Geronimo tree they called it, she'd carried a cantaloupe out there and he'd spoken to her, who they called Geronimo.

I fly east toward the Dragoon Mountains, Cochise Stronghold, Chiricahua National Monument. Much later I'll read the *Autobiography of Geronimo*, how all he wanted in this life was to come home to this place, the blue mountains I drive toward, how the old brave had petitioned the President of the United States, whose house he'd once slept in, and asked to go home, that's all he wanted, to go home. But Great White Father said *no*. And he said *no* again, and again. The last free Indian on the continent collapsed in an Oklahoma ditch, died of pneumonia the next day. Even his bones never got home.

My turn off is announced by a half dozen road signs, gunslingers at the OK Corral, the Boothill Cemetery, a photo of a towel-draped woman getting her back massaged, a wild Indian in war paint riding an Appaloosa, a giant red cowboy boot, a hand-painted billboard saying SEE LIVE TWO-HEADED SNAKE, above twin serpents. A tour bus has pulled over and its passengers are taking turns getting photographed with the signs as backdrop. I skip it, opt for Highway 90, a side road that takes me toward a place called Contention City, where I hit 82 across the San Pedro River, the back way into Tombstone.

Mom Dee and Josephine, Uncle Earl and Buddy, they stand in front of a big stone house in the one photograph I have of where I'm going, if that place even exists. There are trees and shade, a car parked in the dirt, a split rail fence. The sun is hard in their eyes. The Geronimo tree is there, the last run at old Mexico. Freedom and death. My beat up, duct-taped atlas with Arizona on the left and Arkansas on the right, that's all I have to go on. The San Pedro River.

Wouldn't Indians need to follow water? The map takes the river south, just nipping Tucson, down into the Coronado National Monument into Mexico at a place called *Agua Prieta,* dark water.

There's a campground below the bridge, a bathroom that stinks to high heaven, though there's toilet paper, hallelujah. On the stall door someone's written GO HOME.

I say I will. I am. Don't forget the snake. There's a stool at the foot of the wooden man. Uncle Davey'd lifted the head while standing on the stool. *Only the righteous can do this*, he said. *Look.*

Outside the fetid restroom, at a picnic table overlooking the San Pedro, I sip from Jack's water bottle and eat chocolate. A hawk, or is it an osprey, hits the surface of the water, rises with a fish.

Surely I'm way gone now.

The paper is thin, a tag team match, The Angel of Sorrow and Little Lord Fontelbury versus the Comancheros. El Diablo's in the mix. The photo has the young dwarf dressed as an English dandy, a tea cup steaming in his right hand, the pinky pointed outward just so. A headless chicken lays limp between them, the slightest line of blood drips down Otto's chin. What was he thinking, doing that? The thought of it makes me sick, and its with that momentary nausea, the fetid restroom steaming beneath the blue sky and the river ever-running south, that the last of the paper falls from the bundle and I see.

Buddy's dog tags sway from the rearview—they're getting the sun, the dark letters glowing. Six crisp fifties lay inside a graduation card signed by the family— the whole lot of the Washers. They wish Daddy their love, call on him to visit them in Tucson, they'd make the feast for him, make him a home. There are phone numbers and street addresses, rudimentary maps of whole neighborhoods and houses, Xs marking stopover spots. Buddy's written a note in Dad's hand: *Son, You are with me in my heart, you always have been. I'm sorry you never got this—that we never met. Maybe the next world, I'll wait for you there. Look for me, please. We'll find Jo, be a family again. Much love. B/Dad.*

There's a photo, a framed three-by-five of the three of them, Daddy in-between, the one I'd set out to draw by coming here.

That's what this is about, I know now. About a marriage, a family, how what holds some together drives others apart. I don't know this now, but will.

The last thing is a golden ring, a man's ring, inscribed—*love forever, j.*

Story was, Daddy'd swallowed the wedding ring Mom bought him, said, "Now I'm worth thirty-five bucks."

"Sixty," she'd said. "I missed the sale."

They'd come west, held out, made me. That much I know. I slip Buddy's wedding ring over a thumb, *love forever, j.* Josephine. One day another will wear it, and the

J will be for *Jillice*, my middle name, the one I share with Mom, so Dad could have worn it, but he never would touch anything of Buddy's, not ever.

A yellow arrow points to a path worn into the riverside. View Rock Art, a bullet riddled sign says. I hoist the iced cooler into the shade of a front tire, cover it with my day pack. Why not?

The sun-warmed willows smell like the inside of sweat lodge on winter solstice, the intersection of air and earth, fire and water. No sound save the river, *mini wakan*. Holy water, the oldest medicine. I have no watch, my phone's long dead. So I'm not sure what time it is when I walk off with Jack's blue-blue water bottle, away from my car and my suitcase and measly food, my change purse and driver's license and social security card. Up ahead, a shadow slices the willows, and for a second I'm afraid. A river running south through the desert, a holy thing, the life gathered here. The pathway winds with the bank. Deer hooves *V* a waterside crossing. November 14, chill, full snow moon. I wade in to my knees, squat and pee in the river, wash myself. The water's cold, clean. I wash my face, splash underarms, full alert. At the fiesta, the sisters had brought out photos of the ones who'd passed—Vi, Buddy and Josephine, and, finally, one of Daddy as a baby, her holding him, both look into the camera's eye, and the photographer had not tricked him into smiling. Daddy looks bewildered, the lost boy, man at the mouth of the kiva, mother with child.

Apaches trained their children to take a mouthful of river water, run a twenty-mile loop, and return to the very spot, where they had to spit the water back into the river, proof that they'd breathed through their noses for the whole run. Mexicans had killed Geronimo's wife and daughter, his mother, and he swore vengeance on them, learned the medicine way so no bullet would ever kill him, and they gave him his name, screaming *San Gerome* at the ambush, and the word stuck, transformed. He became the word—fear incarnate. Many times they walked this way, this path walked into the earth, I know this now, that I am near their center, the place to get back to or die trying.

I soak a bandana in the river, tie it around my neck, follow the trail over a rise, and see.

There had been a Mexican man at the table, Roberto, Daddy's brother. And a woman, Reina, his sister. They'd only ever seen him as the bewildered baby, he was dead to them, my father. Arkansas was a million miles from Arizona, and that path was erased from the dirt when Buddy walked away from Tucker Prison Farm where he'd been sentenced for impersonating a postman and trying to kidnap Daddy. Chickens come home to roost. Daddy moved to Utah—*twice*. And this is not so far from there, three or four days running for an Apache, the water a burning mouthful.

And I've come back, haven't I?

From a distance, the first thing you see are the trees, big cottonwoods whose leaves have gone bright yellow in the late fall. Golden, they glow from where the river slices flat earth, and it had once been possible to irrigate the field of squash and beans, melons. The ditches are not visible, but they are there, beyond the big cottonwoods waving.

Closer, the rock house, the glint of windowpanes, stone hearth and fireplace, thin smoke rising—is this how it had looked for the walkers? The easy trail down over the rise into the fluvial plain where the San Pedro had flooded millenniums before the gospel fisherman for whom it was named had ever breathed air. The Spanish would have walked this way with Coronado, Escalante, across the Sonora to the Mongolian Rim that would become Apache National Forest. From where I stand, the flood plain seems a good place to stop, rest, beg food and make ready for the next day's run. It's a place to cross the world for, as Josephine had, and from here I can see that the road from the campground at the bridge is the very one that intersects the long driveway that leads to the stone house, which is inhabited. Maybe they're friendly. Maybe they will understand my need, why I come. How this place is bigger than any one or three of us. Who can own it? The thin smoke rising?

On the way back I pass Newspaper Rock, where travelers across the ages have left their marks. There are spirals and petroglyphs of lizards and bighorn, anthromorphs and a pictograph of a woman with a white star inside her belly—star woman. There's a sun shield, a wolf man, Kokopelli laying on his back playing the phallic flute. Bear and wolf prints pock the shadow side, and where a dagger of light shines, the Anasazi fertility symbol I'll one day find along the San Juan cliffs in fall with my people, when the cottonwoods have gone yellow and the river corridor smells of willow and fire.

Vulva or kiva.

Both.

24.

January is named for the god Janus who looks forward and backward at the same time.

That's when I was born, in Utah on a full moon night when crazed women howled, snow flew in the sky, and it was said a woman saved herself from freezing in the Wasatch National Forest by dancing all night. A backward-forward girl woman, what the Lakota call *Heyoka*, kin to the Thunder Beings, *Wakinyan Tanka*, here I am. Sage-scented air rushes through the open window. Across the bridge, on the flood plain of the San Pedro, I fly, the sun at my back, throwing my shadow tall as a house. Not twenty miles from Mexico, I've run far as I can and still stay nineteen. I'm driving fast in a car somewhere in Arizona, on the path of Geronimo, the wind's in my hair and I can see my face in the side view, the yellow flecks in my eyes that I got from Mom and her mom's hazel, which rhymes with *schlimazel*, my bitchy roommates tell me. The widow's peak is from Josephine, I'm carrying her with me as well, Daddy's people on both sides, the ones he knows and the ones he doesn't, the lost sister and brother, the old dwarf, the lamb baby and Buddy and Vi, they're all with me now, twisted into my blood and bone. My dreams last night were of the night of flying geese, the fall the three of us lay on a blanket in the backyard in the dark and watched them fly way up so high the sun lit them still, turned them pink, so they seemed like a flying *V* from Mars, a hoof print zinging from the other world. Maybe they were storks, or pelicans, the mariachis are at it again, a good afternoon to arrive. Everything holy moves in a circle.

Doesn't it?

Geronimo, it was claimed, had the power—*N'daa K'eh Godih*—to suspend time and place. He was said to be able to forestall sunrise or sunset, to make a season come or go at will. When he walked this way, the last thirty-eight free Indians in the United

States, in chase were 5,000 American troops, a quarter of the whole U.S. Army, 3,000 Mexican soldiers and maybe 1,000 bounty hunters, 9,000 armed men in pursuit of 38 Chiricahua, pitifully armed, shoeless and without food. They moved as spirits move, along the thin shining river that runs between space and time. Backward-forward people, medicine spirits. The sage fragrant breath between their lips.

By the time I get to Katy's drive, I know why I've come.

She can see me by my dust. How it rises from the long drive in, along the split rail fence intact on either side. I turn the mariachi music off and drive slow, in silence, touch the cigarette lighter's red eye to Mom's sage bundle, *azilia*, sing *Tunkasila, omaki ya yo,* thank you. The dash clock says three o'clock, then two fifty-nine, two fifty-eight. When I turn the key off the thing's quit altogether, straight up noon flashing on and off. The sage bundle flares. I spit in my left hand, put it out there.

I haul the little cooler out, set it on a shoulder and walk. The wood smoke rises from the ancestral fireplace. I taste it, and there's a chill in the air, a nip, the river-wet bandana cold around my neck. A little cloud flies in, the afternoon sun shining through. The air tastes like snow. The chimney stone was quarried from a hill called Dragon's Back, cut in triangular slabs because the year had a three in it, and there were three of them at first who lived here. The grout is cut with cactus juice and lime, the old Indian secret, the structure is sound, it has held through time. A water hose stretches from a spigot out back, and I fill Jack's water bottle, sweet, cold well water spurting from the dark eye. I drink. And it is good, the water.

I wish that I could say that I heard singing, that the drumbeat reached me and lifted my heart, but that's not true. The tallest of the cottonwoods, the one that shone from a mile away, grows from a flat circle of space where people have gathered, I can tell. There's shade, and the ground's held enough moisture for sweet grass where yellow leaf has fallen, the breeze fresh now, willow on it, river. A couple silver-rimmed clouds sail above, the darkest one covering the sun, though I hadn't known it was cloudy— wasn't the day clear, bright and shining? It's possible to forget, under the cottonwood on the bank of a river in November, the chill come on, hungry, I realize.

My stomach growls.

On new gold leaf, I sit. The ground is very real. From here the house is not close enough to hit with a rock, nor an arrow. Maybe a gunshot. I feel their eyes, no meanness there, fear, yes, fear. It's quiet here, this place of mine.

N'daa K'eh Godih, prayer medicine, time.

Then the snow falls. Fast and furious, like crazy, flakes big as fists and the sun full shining, blazing yellow eyes through the cottonwood leaves. Loop de loop it falls on the circle of earth near the river where a part of my father is said to be buried. I see her then, step down from the stone steps, her eyes bright, the silver blade in her hands—she knows. She comes to me now, we intertwine, backward and forward, again.

In my lap, the cantaloupe is chill against the insides of my thighs. I want to remember her this way, Katy of my dreams, thrum in my blood. Her feet print the freak snow, the sun full out, the devil beating his wife they say in Arkansas. All of that behind us now, the curse broken, the circle sutured shut.

It tickles my face, the snow. Dragon's Back is dark in the distance, the triangles cut from its heart on fire now in the house hearth. Oh Mama and Daddy, I'm sending you this heart message. I've made it. We've made it all the way now. West, the whole way, further even than Rawlins where fringed cowboys galloped firing six-guns with the Medicine Bow at their backs. Down into golden Utah where the sun explodes over the Salt Lake, Zion they call it, heaven on earth, where I was born in January. The bare boned back of the Colorado Plateau, the rivers collide and slice the earth a mile deep and more, until the Vishnu Schist sharp as razors gleams from green water, the Zoroaster Granite, rock not seen light for five-billion years, when the earth was hot and furious and life had not yet drawn its breath. Water, with earth between its teeth, hell bound for what is called Mexico, the Gulf of California, two hundred miles hence.

West.

Toward hope, life, a space and time inhabited for thirty thousand years, more, yellowman come walking with yellow wolf, following camel, giant sloth, woolly mammoth, the great humped buffalo, Clovis points and skinners, the circles of kivas built upon kivas.

The Hopi snake dancers singing for lost white brother, *Pahana*, who one day'd come back so the fourth world could end, only it was the metal-headed Spaniards riding their giant dogs. Sword-bearers, their right hands were never offered palm out and open. *Wachichu*, the one who steals the fat. We came, and kept coming. Killed the buffalo, handed out small pox blankets, the only good Indian is a dead Indian, Crazy Horse, Sitting Bull, Wounded Knee, Gatling gun, all that, sure. Dakota Access Pipeline. Trumpet. Me? Daddy's people have land on the Trail of Tears. The family cemetery's there, on the Trail of Tears, where black-eyed Susan blooms and blackberry grows crazy, where copperheads taste the air with forked tongues and my MaMa Josephine lays buried this second.

The shadow people arrive.

I can't see them so maybe they can't see me, but we're here, in between then and now. The snow melts. Riverside, a fire burns. I smell smoke, the potent aroma of meat cooking. I'm hungry as I've ever been. The bandana is blue-cold around my neck. I'm sitting on cottonwood leaves. I've brought cantaloupe.

All of that behind us now. The curse, the circle.

Remember me this way, love, the cantaloupe cold between my legs, and she who'd crawled down from the old-old hearth about to meet my eyes. Let her come to me now and remember us so when time resumes, the flesh-pink fruit sliced between the lips of thirty-eight ragged Chiricahua, sustenance for this last run toward freedom and death.

Keep trying, Geronimo.

Snow on golden leaf. I am here. I am here. We meet eyes. Love, I am here with you. And when time begins again, the old sun and moon and silver stars newly entwined, I am here with you, before I go.

I was born west, like you, Katy, under the full wolf moon in a January snow, gazing forward and then back, at what has been and will be. And I am here with you, now, the gift cantaloupe waiting to be carved.

Lend me the silver blade. I'll slice half through, take one side as mine, and the other for you.

When I look back on that afternoon in November, when I was nineteen and alone and free for the first time in my life, what'll get me isn't the snow or the golden leaf or the vision of the girl born west like me. It won't be the river or the water hose spurting through one dark eye. Nor the triangles cut from Dragon's Back because the year had a three in it and there were three of us forever—Dad, Mom, me. What I'll remember in my head and heart and that part of me that I've learned is soul, is the bullet riddled sign, View Rock Art, it had said, and pointed to the path walked into the dirt beside the river. For some reason I'd walked that way, I don't know why.

There are a lot of paths in this life, a whole slew of ways to go. But I've come to believe that the ones we're meant to walk, they speak to us the way light speaks sometimes, or water, the feel of a rock in the hand, mud between the toes. I don't know if it's a right way or a wrong way so much as a way of being once you've made the choice, gone this way instead of that. That's what brought us here. That's what brought me here. *This* way instead of *that*.

And that's what will take me home.

The melon is cold. It tastes good. Where had it grown? Under what sky? What mountain?

Whose hands had cut it from the vine, what were they thinking? Had it rained, was the sun shining? Were they hungry or happy or sad or alone. Was family near? Had their story wound and twisted so that bits and pieces of themselves were flung to the wind and one day they'd have to gather themselves to themselves?

The cantaloupe is sweet and good. The sun is out, the snow melted and the afternoon winds out before me. I leave it at the base of the golden cottonwood where my father's birth placenta was buried on a day in January, so that this would be his home, the center of his universe, and it would draw him here and pull him west, one day to this very spot, maybe, where I'm standing when the medicine prayer turns loose of time. Thirty-eight, each with a mouthful of river water, disappear, they run south and are gone.

In the dreams of flight that will bear me through the rest of my life, I'll unfurl condor wings, so they see the white stripe on the underside, and show me their eyes, dark and glinting, hold their right hands palm up, and wish me speed and good medicine.

I'll fly west, wake in the morning before light, the dream fresh on my face as I'm leaving, the windows down and the sun coming over the mountains.

The tree will burn into my mind, my spirit, the tallest cottonwood, I'd see from the rise where the path has taken me. She grows from the circle where we gathered, her skin in layers, she has sipped the air of centuries into her veins, turned the years into carbon, so that her body holds within its flesh our life's breath and memory. Geronimo is there, his father, his mother, mine. The girl whose skin was sewn into the pouch around his neck on that distant afternoon when Katy crawled down and broke bread with Indians. How many rings in the tree's heart back to Josephine when she carried Daddy here to bury the sage-wrapped umbilical cord and the caul that had covered his face? How many to me and the one who comes after?

Where rattlesnakes dance in their dens, the roots run down, branch under the river and run like mouthfuls of water spat from a mouth that says the prayer medicine words so time is turned loose. And I'll wait for a moment in that space in between, that holy not-knowing place. The sun will turn red, and that redness will bruise the sky from here to forever and then be dark. Today is a Monday, full snow moon, the nearest to earth in eight years. It will rise over Dragon's Back and throw my shadow ten feet tall. In my bones I feel her pull.

I walk away from the tallest cottonwood. Stepping in moonlight, I've left something of myself in the breath of the mother tree.

Geronimo paratroopers cried as they as they leapt from airplanes over battlefields where the bomb-dwarfed moon flowers bloomed and they fell toward the rest of their lives.

Geronimo.

I'm breathing the word, falling home.

About the Author

Michael Gills is the author of eight books of fiction and nonfiction, including the novel *Emergency Instructions* (Raw Dog Screaming Press, 2017) and short story collection *The House Across From The Deaf School* (Texas Review Press, 2016) which was nominated for the PEN/Faulkner Prize for Fiction and won the 15 Bytes Utah Book Prize. Other work has won the *Southern Humanities Review*'s Theodore Hoefner Prize for Fiction, the *Southern Review*'s Best Debut of the Year, recognition in the Pushcart Prize Anthology, inclusion in *New Stories From The South: The Year's Best*, and numerous Utah Arts Book Prizes. His undergraduate novel writing workshop has been featured in USA Today, and several of his students have gone on to publish books of their own. Gills teaches for the Honors College at the University of Utah, where he lives in the foothills with his wife, Jill.

www.ingramcontent.com/pod-product-compliance
Lightning Source LLC
Chambersburg PA
CBHW030515260626
47157CB00005B/1755